I0671618

Tempus: A Dezeray Jackson Novel

Sinfully Scandalous Mysteries, Volume 3

Kori D. Miller

Published by Back Porch Writer Press, 2020.

TEMPUS: A DEZERAY JACKSON NOVEL

First edition. July 31, 2020.

ISBN: 978-1540134479

Written by Kori D. Miller.

Also by Kori D. Miller

A Dezeray Jackson Short Read
Deadly Sins I
Deadly Sins II
Deadly Sins III

Sinfully Scandalous Mysteries
Hush: A Dezeray Jackson Novel
North Downing: A Dezeray Jackson Novel
Tempus: A Dezeray Jackson Novel

Standalone
My Life in Black and White

Watch for more at https://www.koridmiller.com.

For my family. You tell me the right things, at the right time, to snap me out of the sticky spots I find myself.

Chapter One

"LOOK, I KNOW HOW YOU feel, he's a complete dumbass." Hands raised chest high, I inched closer to her. "But you can't," The pop, pop from her nine millimeter sent me scrambling for cover behind a white, floor-to-ceiling pillar. I never understood rich people's fascination with Roman architecture in their overly sized living rooms. "You can't kill him. Just put the gun down. Do you really want to spend the rest of your life in prison because of his sorry ass?"

The man in question had the good sense to cower behind one of two plush sofas in the room. Mary Beth Reynolds stood in the entryway with the gun, and her eyes, trained on her husband. Sirens blared in the distance.

"Do you hear that? You don't want to be holding that gun when the police get here." Mary Beth lowered her arms, apparently thinking about what I'd said, but in an instant, they rose, and she fired another shot. Dumbass had made a move toward a door. The bullet ricocheted off the side of a bookcase and grazed his arm. He yelped, grabbing his arm with his other hand. All things considered; it could have been much worse.

"Got ya!" She said.

"This isn't High Noon! Put the gun down!"

She shrugged and set the gun onto a nearby table.

Two police officers entered through the front door, guns drawn. A third appeared from a hallway behind me.

"Step away from the weapon!" He ordered; gun trained on Mary Beth.

I looked over at Pat Reynolds. Blood dripped from his arm to the white carpet.

"You're bleeding on the carpet!" Mary Beth's shrill voice rose above the officer's commands. Pat Reynolds hit the floor like a sack of corn feed in a truck bed. His head just missed a round, stone table near the French doors that almost gave him his freedom.

As the police took control of the scene, I stepped out into what had turned into a brisk evening. The day had started with sunshine and mild temps, but now fall was making its way into the plains. I walked toward the driveway.

"Jackson, what the hell are you doing here?" Detective Halliday had just arrived.

"Finishing up a case, that's all."

"Why is it your cases always end up with someone shooting somebody?"

"Good question. I'll get back to you when I figure that out." I headed down the path to my Jeep.

"Where do you think you're going? We need your statement."

By the time Officer Jacobs took my statement, it was eleven o'clock, and I knew trouble was waiting for me at home. Leaving my Rottie, Godfrey, cooped up all day, never usually ended well.

The drive from the Reynolds' place to mine normally took ten minutes, but I stopped at Hy-Vee to get Godfrey a peace offering. A couple butcher bones, and a small ribeye would do the trick. He was finicky, but reasonable. My last meal was lunch, so I grabbed some pre-made sushi rolls, a couple beers, and water.

Evening, Dez." Susie greeted me at the checkout. "You're early tonight."

Stopping in for a late-night snack had been the norm for me since catching the Reynolds case a month ago.

"Someone's gonna be pretty happy to see these." She set the bones into a plastic bag.

"You'd think."

"Hey, I've been meaning to ask you something."

"Shoot."

"My sister has been seeing this guy." She continued scanning, not making eye contact as she slid each item across the scanner and into a bag. "He's married."

An involuntary sigh escaped. What is it with women and married men? He's cheating with you. He will never leave his wife. And if he does, he will cheat on you. It makes no sense. I tuned back into Susie who hadn't skipped a beat.

"Anyway, she's pregnant and not sure what she should do. I mean, can she make him pay child support?"

That 'tell me anything' sign on my forehead was on again, flashing big and bright. The trouble is it rarely turns off; it only dims. Everyone and their mother seem to think I know more about legal shit than they do just because I'm a PI. How the hell would I know anything about child support. I ain't got no kids. Don't want any. And I don't date worthless, cheat on your ass, men. But I've got that sign on my forehead. It's very inviting.

"You know what, Susie, I'm not sure. Maybe you could tell her to ask a lawyer. Someone at Legal Aid might know something about that."

"Oh, yeah. That's a great idea. Thanks!"

"No problem. Have a good night." I grabbed my bags quick before she could ask me anything else.

BEFORE MY KEY ENTERED the lock, I could hear Godfrey whining behind the door. Groceries nestled in the crook of my other arm, I pushed against the door, nudging it open against his massive body.

"Come on, Godfrey, you've got to move back." His nose, followed by his shoulders, jammed into the crack between the door and the frame. As I shoved the door open wider, his head smacked the screen door on his way out into the yard. I set my leather messenger bag and keys onto the hall table before walking to the kitchen at the back of the house.

I'd lost what little appetite I had, so I put everything into the fridge. Godfrey scratched at the back door. Normally, I'd think nothing of it, but he shouldn't have been able to get back there from the front. I turned off the kitchen lights to get a better view of the yard. Godfrey's scratching became louder and more insistent. Just in case there was an unwanted surprise waiting for me outside, I grabbed an old wooden cane I kept near the door, before letting Godfrey inside.

If I hadn't had my house broken into repeatedly in the past year, and my door set on fire, I wouldn't think twice about the dog getting into the backyard. I might assume that in one of my moments of exhaustion these past few nights, I'd left the gate open. But I never leave the gate open. Stepping out onto the deck, I surveyed the landscape before descending the stairs. The gate, hidden behind an overgrown evergreen that needed to be dead, was several feet from the lower patio. I did a quick check of the sliding door. Still locked. Then, cane at the ready, walked around the bush, and ran smack into Murphy.

"What the fuck are you doing here?"

"Whoa," He held his hands high. "I just got back."

"Is there some reason you couldn't come through the front door?"

"I was going to, but I wanted to park my bike back here."

I looked over at his Harley.

"Why didn't I hear you?"

"I shut it off and walked it back. I wanted to surprise you." He said this like it was a completely logical thing to do. I stared at him, head cocked to one side, shaking it in disbelief. "Let's get inside," he said.

"What's the hurry?"

"Nothing, really, but you know, it's late."

"What's going on, Murphy? You've been MIA for months. Again."

"Come on babe, let's talk inside." His voice softened to make the request more palatable.

It's not in my nature to take orders. Chalk it up to too much time around my retired military father. Murphy, on the other hand, was accustomed not only to receiving but also following them. I turned back toward the house and could hear Godfrey by the time we reached the bottom of the stairs.

Inside, Murphy tossed the bag he'd been carrying over his shoulder onto a chair. Godfrey scrutinized it, then decided it had nothing he wanted, so he settled on his bed near the basement door. I returned my cane to its spot, then sat at the table.

"Got any beer?"

"In the fridge. Grab me one, too." I said, waiting for an explanation. This is how it always played out with Murphy. He'd stick around for a while, then I'd wake some morning, and he'd be gone. No note. No phone calls. He was former military. I never knew all the details of what he did, but it usually involved extended stays elsewhere with people I was certain I didn't want to know.

He handed me the beer and sat opposite me at the small table. "How've you been?"

"Really? We're gonna do that now?"

"What?" He shrugged.

"Let's see... I just watched some crazy rich lady try to gun down her cheating husband. So that's normal, I guess. Oh, and I finally took a much-needed vacation,"

"Where to?"

"Nowhere. I don't do vacations. You plan on telling me what the hell you've been doing the past few months?"

"A job came up, that's all. You know how it is."

"Hmm. Yeah, right."

"Come on, Dez." He reached for my hand, catching it before I could move it away. "If I could tell you, I would. My clients appreciate discretion, you know that." His fingers stroked the inside of my wrist. I snatched my hand away, stood, and left the kitchen, beer in hand. A few minutes later, I returned.

"Here." I set blankets and a pillow onto the table. "You can sleep on the couch."

Godfrey followed me back into the living room and upstairs, plopping down outside my door as I closed it.

GODFREY'S BARKING WOKE me at six a.m. I stumbled out of bed, rubbed sleep out of my eyes, and opened the bedroom door expecting to see him. As I descended the stairs, he barked, again. This time I could tell he was outside, and I heard Murphy rattling around in the kitchen.

"Morning, babe. Hungry?"

"It's six in the morning. No, I'm not hungry, I'm tired." I opened the door for Godfrey. "Stop making so much damn noise." I left the kitchen, Godfrey trailing behind, and returned to my bedroom. Crawling beneath the covers, I cursed Murphy and buried my head in my pillow.

At nine o'clock, I rolled out of bed, showered, and changed into jeans, a hunter green mock turtleneck, and slid on my black motorcycle boots. To tame my unruly dark curls, I pulled them back into a low tail. I'm a minimalist in the make-up department. A little foundation and some tinted lip balms were about as fancy as I usually got unless it was a special occasion. For those rare events, I added blush and eye shadow.

I stepped over Godfrey on my way out of the room and headed back downstairs. Take two, except Murphy was gone. My office, to the right at the bottom of the stairs, had a note taped to the door. *"See you later tonight. Have to take care of something. Won't be too late."* Crumbling it, I tossed it into the garbage on my way to the kitchen. Godfrey followed close behind. Not knowing if Murphy fed him, I tossed some food into his bowl, set it outside, and he barreled past me.

On my way out the door, I grabbed my bag, keys, and leather jacket. This is Nebraska, where the weather is fickle. My primary objective this morning was to get caught up with my assistant, Clive Dixon. I'd hired him earlier in the year mostly to keep him from returning to his old habits and away from Katrina, my on again, off again best friend. Our relationship is complicated mainly because she controls the Omaha drug trade, and I have a problem with her life choice. But Clive has potential. He's the only member of his family to graduate from high school, and he did it with honors. His oldest brother, Detrick, finally landed in the Pen. That's a long, uninteresting story. He deserves the extended stay the judge gave him.

Clive liked to work out of Do Space off 72nd and Dodge Street. Having missed the morning rush, getting there from my place would take about ten minutes. I knew exactly where I'd find him. Clive was partial to an area near the back, sort of tucked away from most of the action. It was busier than I expected, with almost every computer terminal occupied as I walked through the room to find him.

Clive sat on a long Ikea-type couch, hunched forward, pecking away at his keyboard fast and furious.

"Clive?" No answer. "Clive."

Startled, he looked up.

"Ms. D!" A smile stretched across his face, and he leaned back, slouching against the couch. "I was just finishing up the report for the Castille case."

I took a seat next to the couch, setting my bag on the floor. The Castille case hadn't ended well for any of the parties involved. The Castilles hired me to locate their estranged sixteen-year-old daughter. The girl followed her twenty-five-year-old boyfriend to Miami, my old stomping grounds. By the time I found her, she was dead, and the police had arrested her boyfriend. The girl's father was so distraught, he shot himself, and now his wife is alone raising their other two children.

"When you're finished with that, here are the notes for the Reynolds case." I reached into my bag to get the file.

"What happened?"

I explained Mary Beth Reynold's meltdown and Clive started laughing.

"That woman is crazy. All she could think about was the carpet?"

I nodded.

"I ain't never gettin' married, that's for damn sure."

"Give it time, Clive. You're not even legal to drink, yet."

"That's not what my ID says."

"I didn't hear you say that."

A roaming robot with a screen for a head rolled past, momentarily distracting us both.

"That's just creepy," Clive said. "It's probably recording everything we all do in here. I should find an alternative place to set up."

"There's always the public library."

"Nah, too quiet. I need a little background noise while I concentrate."

"Scooters?"

"I hate coffee."

"Then I guess you're stuck with this place."

"Ya know, you could be like a real investigator and get an office so clients could find you better."

I punched him in the arm.

"Oh, really? They don't seem to have any trouble finding me the way things are now. Besides, the only reason I can pay you is 'cause I keep my overhead low."

"I was just thinking a nice spot near downtown would be perfect."

"And I suppose you have something in mind?"

"Detrick's old warehouse."

I gave him my best "as if" look, rolling my eyes for added effect.

"Clive, no one who wants to hire a PI is going to venture to that part of town to find me. I think you're forgetting that most of our clients are White."

"Hey, with all the fresh development that direction, the warehouse will be part of the action in no time. Better to get in before there's no space left for you."

He had a point. Working from my home office and Zio's Pizzeria was getting a little old. But I didn't want to pay rent somewhere either.

"What's Detrick planning to do with the building?"

"Haven't asked. It's been empty since he went down."

"It's a lot more space than I'd ever need."

"Yeah, but you could rent space to other people."

"I'm not in the landlord business."

"I could manage it for you."

Clive was ambitious. That was one reason I hired him. He could read people almost better than me, and that's a skill some people just don't have and can never develop.

"I don't think so, Clive."

"What? You don't think I got the skills?"

"I know you could do it, I'm just not sure it's what I'd want you to do. You can't manage a building and work as my assistant."

A smile crept across his face. He leaned forward, his forearms resting on his knees. "So, what you're sayin' is that you can't live without my assistant expertise?"

"Something like that, Clive. Listen, I've got to get going."

"You headin' to the gas station gig?"

I nodded and then stood to leave.

"Think about the building, Ms. D. It's an opportunity waiting to happen."

I gave him a backhanded wave as I walked away.

Chapter Two

I WAS ON MY WAY TO meet up with the owner of several local gas stations. Recently, he learned that his inventory was getting depleted, but the sales didn't match up. He wanted me to find out what, or who, was messing with his money. This was more of a discovery meeting because I wasn't sure I wanted to work for him. He had a habit of getting media attention for all the wrong reasons. His most recent PR slip was instructing his employees not to allow kids to linger around the store. On the surface this seemed reasonable until people noticed that tinted kids were the only ones not welcomed inside.

Tom Kincade owned five stations, mostly in and around northwest Omaha. That part of Omaha is a mix of working and middle-class Whites and Blacks, with a few other minorities and refugees slowly changing the landscape. One of his stations wasn't too far from the dojang where I train several times a week, but I didn't fill up my tank there. I avoided all his stations and was surprised when I received his call.

The clerk behind the counter was helping a customer when I entered. Her long, intricately decorated nails clicked the counter as she picked up, and then scanned each item. She'd wrapped her hair in a multicolored scarf that showed off her flawless skin. I would have guessed her to be around twenty-five, but Black people age well, so I could have been off by ten years for all I knew. Her name tag read, Latrice. She gave me a brief head nod and continued what she was doing.

This was the same station that not so long ago was the scene of a deadly shooting, so my Spidey Senses were on full alert. Out of all the possible job choices, convenient store cashier is on my list as one of the most dangerous, that and being a bank clerk. I don't go into banks.

Latrice finished with her customer, then greeted me with a smile.

"Good morning, ma'am. How may I help you?"

She wasn't from around here. No one born and raised in Nebraska ever called me "ma'am." Her accent told me she came from the south, but I couldn't place where. My guess was Georgia or maybe Louisiana, but that was only because so many people moved to Nebraska after Katrina. Now, running into someone from the south seemed commonplace.

"Hi, Latrice. I'm here to meet with Tom."

"Oh, Mr. Kincade? He's in the office, in the back there." Her long, perfect for piano-playing fingers directed me toward the back of the store.

"Thank you."

"Have a wonderful day!"

The office door was closed, but I could hear Kincade speaking on the phone, so I waited before knocking. When it was clear that the conversation had ended, I tapped on the door.

"Mr. Kincade, it's Dezeray Jackson."

"Come in and close the door behind you."

As a general rule, when entering a compact space with an unknown male, I don't close the door behind me, especially when the unknown male has a history of angry outbursts. It's always better to have a straightforward escape route. I left the door slightly ajar.

"I'm sure no one will disturb us," I said and took the seat opposite his metal desk. "You mentioned during our call that you've got concerns about your inventory?"

"Yeah, you could say that." He had a gravelly voice from what I suspected came from years of smoking. His round belly touched the edge of the desk. "Look, Jackson, you came recommended to me by Dick Swan. The only reason I'm not using him is because he's laid up in the hospital."

Dick Swan was a former Omaha police detective who went private after being asked to retire. He and I had crossed paths several months ago when I was working another case.

"How can I help you?"

"This store isn't the problem. Latrice, you probably saw her out front, has been with me a long time, and she handles the inventory. The problem is with two of my other stores further west on Maple."

"The one near 90th Street?"

He nodded and continued. "The other one is over off of Ida."

"How many employees work in those locations?"

"I've got five covering each location. All part time."

Of course, he only hires part-time employees. He probably only pays minimum wage, too. I felt compelled to raise my fee.

"Are there items that are consistently missing?"

"No. It's more like a little of this and a little of that, so they don't get caught. You know, the stuff you could sell out of your trunk. They take a few bags of something here, then a box of something there. Whoever's doing it, it's got to be more than one. They'd have to know someone at both stores."

"But no alcohol or cigarettes?"

"No, none of that."

"When did you notice it was happening?"

He scratched his head and leaned back in his chair, causing it to creak. I wasn't entirely sure it could support his weight.

"When the Maple store was closed, I had time to dig into the books." His phone chimed and he swiped right, dismissing the notification. "Not me so much. I had Latrice do it. She's the one who figured it out."

He slid a piece of notebook paper across the desk. "These are the names of my employees at those stores. Their schedules, contact information, and addresses are all there. What's this gonna cost me, Jackson?"

I thought about that for a beat, knowing what I planned to charge him, but wanted to appear like I was taking things into consideration.

"Five thousand up front plus expenses."

"Five thousand! I could see paying Swan that kind of money, but you? The only reason I'm even interested in you is because you're one of them. I'll give you two."

I stood to leave and was part way out the door

"Wait, fine. I'll give you four, but that's it."

I turned back. "Mr. Kincade, my fee for this situation is five thousand plus expenses. If you're not prepared to pay for that today, then you're more than welcome to find someone else. Maybe someone a bit more like yourself."

He pulled a business checkbook from a drawer, scrawled the amount, signed it, and then tossed it across the desk. It landed on top of the notebook paper. I reached for both and slid them into the side pocket of my satchel.

"I'll be in touch." I left, already feeling conflicted. There are always people who hire me who I know are bigots, but it's a distinct feeling when it's blatant. Something about in-your-face down-home racism is both comforting and unsettling. I think it's because you know where you stand with those kinds of people. I'd like to say I'd never work for them, but since it's nearly impossible to avoid, I just charge them more.

THE FIRST PERSON ON Kincade's list worked at the location near 90th & Maple streets. The guy's name was Abdul, and his shift was almost over when I arrived. I parked in the lot not too far from the entrance. The next employee had just stepped behind the counter. She was about five foot two inches tall at the most. They exchanged pleasantries, then Abdul headed outside with a backpack slung over one shoulder, and got into a dark blue, four-door Buick. I made a note of that. A few minutes later, when his car engine wouldn't turn over, I pulled my Jeep next to his.

"Need a jump?" I'd rolled down my passenger window.

"Yeah, that'd be great. Thanks."

I popped the hood and stepped out, cables in hand.

"Here."

We got everything hooked up. One try, and his car was up and running, again.

"Thanks, you really saved my ass. I've got to get to class."

"Hey, no problem. You go to UNO?"

"Yeah, psych major. Thanks, again. I need to jet."

Tossing the cables onto my backseat, I locked the Jeep and entered the store. Several customers came and went. Some paying for gas, others buying lunch. When there seemed to be a lull in the traffic, I stepped to the counter.

"Can I get a job application?"

The young woman looked at me skeptically, reached beneath the counter, and produced a generic application.

"The pay sucks," she said before handing it to me. Her name was Tonya, according to the tag on her uniform.

"Gotta eat."

"True enough."

"You worked here long?"

"About six months. The owner's a dick."

"Why stay?"

"It's walking distance from my apartment, I ain't got a car, and I don't want to work at Mickey D's."

"Do you know if he's looking for any more help?"

"He's always looking. The turnover here is atrocious. I'm constantly having to cover somebody's ass."

"That's good though. I mean, more hours, more money."

"Sure, but a girl's gotta have a life, too."

A few customers had entered and were queuing up behind me. Tonya looked past me to the next person in line.

"May I help you?"

I grabbed the application and returned to my Jeep.

ALL THOSE PEOPLE COMING into Kincade's place in search of a quick lunch reminded me I hadn't had mine, yet. I'm a devout consumer of thin crust, cracker-like pizza, and when I can't get it the way I like it, thin is the only absolute requirement. That, and it needs to taste good. I pointed my Jeep toward Zio's Pizzeria on Dodge Street. My timing was perfect because I'd missed the lunch rush and was there before the early dinner crowd. A server directed me to a booth, giving me a view of the parking lot. Before I reached the safety of my table, I heard, "Dez?"

I turned and saw Susie from HyVee. Apparently, she'd walked in after me.

"Hi, Susie. How's it going?" No one ever expects a genuine answer to this question, but I've learned over many years that when I ask it, I almost always get one. The problem is, I can't think of anything else to ask when you bump into someone you barely know.

"Not so great."

There's the bait. I had two choices — I could pretend I didn't hear it and respond with a generic "Sorry to hear that. I'm sure things will get better," and excuse myself, or be a sincere human being.

"Sorry to hear,"

"That guy my sister is seeing, you know, the one I told you about? Anyway, he's such an asshole. Can you believe he told her to get rid of it? That's what he called the baby. An 'it.'"

"Uh, huh. Sorry to,"

"I keep telling her to stand up to him. Honestly, she really should tell his wife, but she keeps making excuses for him. He will never leave his wife, but Libby, that's my sister, she doesn't believe me."

I stood there nodding and listening, all the while hearing my stomach rumble every time a slice of pizza zoomed past me to someone's table.

"Listen, Susie, I'm in kind of in a rush. I'm sorry to hear about your sister, but I'm sure she'll figure it all out. Best you can do is stay out of it."

"I tried, but I can't. She's my sister."

"I understand. Really, I do. It's hard to watch someone you care about make a mistake, but that's on them. You know what I mean? She's an adult."

"She's only nineteen."

That got my attention.

"Um, how old is this guy we're talking about?"

"I don't know. I think he's in his forties."

I cranked my head back and forth to loosen the tightening in my neck.

"How'd she meet him?"

"She's a student at UNO. I think they met at some event a few months ago. He doesn't work for the university, though. She said he's some hot shot researcher or something. I don't know. All I do know is that he's an asshat."

"Fair enough."

"What should I tell her to do?"

"Susie, you really can't do anything. It doesn't sound like your sister will listen to you."

"She might listen to you."

"Why in the world would she do that? She doesn't even know me."

"Yeah, but maybe you could find some dirt on him. She'd have to listen then."

"In my experience, that doesn't always matter. Besides, she was willing to get involved with him even though she knew he was married."

"She didn't know until after she told him about the baby."

"What?"

"He was lying to her the whole time. What if he's lying about something else? She'd have to see him for what he really is. Don't you think?"

"No. She's in love. That alone makes her unreliable."

I could see tears forming in her eyes. I hate that.

"Do you have his name?"

"Rick Castle. Will you help me?"

"I can't make any promises, and I'm swamped with other cases." That wasn't entirely true, but since this was likely to be a pro bono situation, I thought it prudent to keep her expectations low.

"No, no, of course, I understand. I'm just relieved that you'll try. Thanks, Dez. You're amazing."

I left without my pizza. There was no way I would stay and eat. Susie would have expected me to invite her to sit with me, and I wasn't in the mood to share my space. Sometimes pizza needs to be a singular experience.

Chapter Three

ON MY WAY TO KINCADE'S store off Ida Street, I stopped at a Casey's gas station to grab a snack. I was starving, which naturally led to a few poor choices; A can of Pringles, a Coke, and a Snickers somehow followed me back into my Jeep. Already feeling guilty, I tossed them onto the passenger seat. Then, I reminded myself that it was Susie's fault that I didn't eat a decent lunch, and I felt much better.

By the time I arrived at Kincade's, the Pringles and Snickers were a memory, but the Coke and its burn lingered. I eased into a spot at the far-right of the entrance. A large dumpster, partially hidden behind a lattice fence, sat further back from the primary parking area. Two white males near it appeared to be arguing. One man had a tattoo on his right forearm that I couldn't quite make out. He stood back from the taller man, who made sweeping gestures with his hands, and then pointed at the other guy's chest. I lowered my window.

"I told you not to do it, man. This shit is real and I'm not taking a hit for you." The taller man pushed his long bangs from his face and flipped his hair all to the left.

"Stop worrying. You always worry too much."

The taller guy didn't seem reassured by that and started pacing. Tattoo guy spoke, again.

"Listen, as long as we keep doing what we're doing, everything will be fine. No one ain't gonna know. All you have to do is show up." He rested his hand on the taller man's shoulder. "Trust me."

The taller man shoved the hand off, turned, and walked away, heading toward the bus stop at the corner. The guy with the tat grabbed a skateboard that'd been leaning against the building, hopped on, and sped past my Jeep. The crackle of the wheels rolling over the pavement faded into the distance.

When I entered the store, the place was empty except for a female cashier.

"Did you hear all that?" I asked.

"Hear what? What you talking about?"

"Two guys were out by the dumpster arguing. It looked like they were about to throw down."

"Shit, that's just Randy and Tate. They always arguing ever since I been here."

"How long has that been?"

"A few months. Why? What's it got to do with you?"

"I was thinking 'bout picking up an application, but maybe I don't want to work with crazy."

"They ain't crazy. Stupid as fuck sometimes, but not crazy. Most of the time their antics are entertaining." She reached beneath the counter and produced a job application. "Here, but honestly you need to know that the hours and pay suck."

"Who owns this place?"

"A dude named Tom Kincade." Her name tag read, "Chantelle."

"Oh, isn't he the guy who was in the news a while back. Something about not serving Blacks?"

"We work for him, but he doesn't want us in his store buying his crap. It makes no sense, but then when has any racist mo'fo ever made any sense?"

"Why you working here?" I asked, folding the application.

"No vehicle to get around and ain't riding no damn bus all over town for pay not much better than this. 'Sides, this is the devil I know."

I shrugged. Couldn't argue with that logic. I thanked Chantelle for the application, words of caution, and left.

The Coke was bogging down my insides and making me feel sluggish, so I made my way over to Simmons Martial Arts Academy for a quick workout. I always keep extra gear and clothes in my Jeep. This wasn't the best time to stop into the dojang because the after-school kids would start their classes. soon But, I figured I could always do some bag work in the back.

An hour and a half later, freshly showered, with my curls air drying, I said goodbye to Master Simmons and stepped outside. The sun was setting, and the air temperature had dropped. I zipped up my leather jacket to guard against a slow chill creeping up my back and tossed my gym bag onto the backseat of my Jeep. Snapping my seatbelt, I contemplated going home, but knew there wasn't anything worth eating in my refrigerator, and Godfrey was outside.

Since I was denied my favorite lunch food, I decided I'd indulge in my second favorite and knew exactly where to get it.

THE SATISFYING AROMA of grilled meat and fries greeted me as I entered Eddy's Billiard Hall. I sighed deeply and smiled. This place was like coming home except more crowded and with an opportunity to earn some easy bank.

"What's up Ms. D.?" Mack, one of Eddy's bouncers waved me through not bothering to check my ID.

"Same shit, different day, Mack. How's the wife?"

"All good, all good."

"Any low hangin' fruit tonight?"

"Back corner. Fools won't see you comin.' Been boozin' since four o'clock. I'd say they're ripe."

I made my way to the end of the bar where I saw Eddy mixing drinks. His fitted black T-shirt gave away his muscular physique and said, "Don't" on the back.

"Well, well, if it isn't little Ms. D." The front of his shirt was blank which left me wondering what the hell "don't" meant.

"Hey, Eddy. Feeling philosophical this evening?" I pointed at his shirt.

"Always, baby girl. Where you been hiding? Hang on, let me just get these youngins their poison."

Swiveling my seat around, I surveyed the playing arena. That table in the back left definitely needed my attention, but there were a few other viable options. If only I had a few clones.

"Aw right, now." Eddy returned with a beer and water for me. "You want your usual? I'm assuming you're here this early to eat, not just to take people's money and run."

"Thanks, and yeah I'll take my usual."

"Good, 'cause I already put the order in. So, back to the question of the evening. Where have you been? You haven't stopped in for what, a few weeks at least."

"Lots of cases, and I'm still training Clive."

"Uh, huh. How's that working out?" He leaned against the back bar; arms folded across his chest.

"He's sharp. Lots of potential."

"Tracer material?"

"Maybe, but he's too young. They won't even look at him until he's twenty-one."

"Yo, big man! Can we get some service, or what?" A stout, college-age guy and his buddies stood at the opposite end of the bar.

Eddy's right eyebrow raised, and his jaw tightened. He took a deep breath.

"Service here sucks. Yo, big man, we'd like a few beers."

Mack stood from his perch at the door.

Eddy cranked his head left, then right, and said, "Sit tight." He walked from behind the counter and in a few quick steps was smack in front of the kid and his crew. Eddy towered over half of them. It was apparent that they didn't realize how big Eddy was until that moment. Two of them backed up and into Mack. The loudmouth stood his ground.

"Get out."

"You can't,"

Eddy grabbed Loudmouth by the front of his shirt, picked him up, and said one more time, "Get out."

His friends had already left and customers closest to the action stopped what they were doing. No one disrespected Eddy in his place, or anywhere else for that matter. I'd known Eddy a long time. He and my father served together, and it was Eddy who taught me everything I know about guns and shooting pool. After my sister Savannah was murdered, I'd spent a lot of hours in this hall. Clearly this kid was new.

Eddy set him down closer to the door. Loudmouth turned, ran into Mack's chest, and stumbled back into Eddy. Mack grabbed the kid and escorted him out. The offender gone; people returned to their pool games like nothing happened.

I stuck around until about ten o'clock and pocketed a few hundred before saying my goodbyes to Eddy and Mack. Exhaustion had taken over and all I wanted to do was crawl beneath my down comforter and sleep.

MURPHY WAS ON THE COUCH sleeping with the TV on and Godfrey asleep on the floor next to him. I kicked off my shoes, hung up my jacket, and dropped my satchel onto the table near the grandfather clock. Godfrey's head raised a little, then flopped back down when he realized it was me. I removed my jeans and slung them over the back of a chair, then slid in next to Murphy. He stirred.

"Babe? What time is it?"

"After ten-thirty."

"Hmm." He kissed me slowly, and then deeply. It was one of those lingering kisses that invites you to settle in for a while. Murphy's hands made their way to my breasts, caressing them before finding their way to my panties. He moved me beneath him, and I helped him get out of his boxers. It'd been months since we'd last seen or touched each other. The warmth of his body against mine, the weight of him, it all felt right. The months apart hadn't affected Murphy's memory for what I liked. Satisfied, we curled up together, and I fell into a dreamless sleep.

Chapter Four

I KNOW IT'S IMPORTANT to perform my civic duty, but a jury summons is like disappearing into a black hole. There's no other way to describe it. You sit for hours with nothing to do but twiddle your thumbs, and maybe talk to someone interesting, while waiting to see if you'll get chosen for a jury. This can take all day. Then, if you're selected, you're stuck with no way out.

This is what I kept thinking about during my week-long, forced internship with horrible pay. That, and the fact that my case wasn't getting any traction. It wasn't as if I could hand the Kincade case off to Clive. The minimal surveillance I'd had him do so far was with me, mostly because he's only nineteen and I'm not ready to let him leave the nest. He'd be happy to take on more responsibility.

It was Friday, and in a few scant hours, I'd be on my way out the door never to return — at least not until the next summons. I sat outside on steps sequestered from the other jurors so I could catch up on email. A gentle breeze induced a cascade of leaves that swirled through the air before settling to the ground. Days like this reminded me why I returned to Nebraska. That, and the pull of the free house gifted to me by my aunt Violet.

"Ms. Jackson?"

I turned and looked up from my phone.

"I'm Trevor Hudson." He extended his hand. "Do you have a minute?"

I nodded, and he sat on the step next to me.

"I'm curious if you'd be interested in taking on a few cases with my law firm from time to time."

I've always appreciated a lawyer who cuts to the chase, but I knew nothing about this man other than he had a disarmingly attractive smile, and a nice build hidden beneath an off the rack suit.

"Your firm?"

"Hudson, Kilpatrick & Associates. We represent young people who've had the misfortune of getting caught up in the system."

"Uh huh, so lots of pro bono stuff."

"Some, yes, but not all. We also represent clients involved in corporate litigations."

"Gotta pay the bills somehow." I smiled.

"We'd like to put you on retainer for the next few months. We're working with a family whose son was killed by a local business owner. You probably saw it in the news."

I shrugged, still unsure who he was talking about. Keeping track of local killings wasn't on the top of my to do list.

"We need someone with your — skill set."

"There are dozens of PIs in Omaha with my skill set."

"Yes, and no."

So much for being a straight shooter.

"The business owner has a fondness for fair-skinned black females."

"That's not a skill set."

"It might make it easier for you to get close to him."

"And why would I need to get close to him?"

"He has a tight inner circle, and we need someone who can gain his trust."

"Who's the business owner?"

"Deacon Faulkner."

"That guy's family owns half the buildings down here." I gestured to the buildings surrounding the courthouse.

"Are you interested?"

Of course, I was interested. Retainers offered a consistent and reliable source of income. Who doesn't want more money in their investment accounts? I retrieved a business card from my back pocket.

"I'll be in touch soon." He handed me his card and stood to leave. Checking his watch, he added, "You better get back in there."

IT FELT GOOD TO GET back into my cases Saturday morning. I had notes left to clean-up before handing them off to Clive, and employees to stalk in the Kincade case. I spent the first several hours of the morning getting organized and planning. At around eleven a.m., my office phone rang, jarring me from the case notes that had been my focus.

"Dezeray Jackson Investigations."

"Dez?" There was an audible sniff, and then, "She's dead."

"Who is this?"

"Su — Susie."

"Are you all right? What happened?"

"My sister. They say she committed suicide. I - I didn't know who else to call."

"Suicide?"

"It—It's ridiculous." She blew her nose. "She would never do that."

"When did this happen?"

"Last night."

"What am I supposed to do? She's all I had. Our parents died a few years ago. She's." Her voice trailed off. Then I heard more sniffing and nose blowing.

"Susie?"

"Uh, huh?"

"Just take it one step at a time. Today, you need to make arrangements for her service."

"Yeah, I know, I know. And I need to write an obituary."

I spent the next fifteen minutes helping Susie make a list of what she needed to do to plan for her sister's funeral. In the end, she decided cremation and a memorial service would be what her sister would want. After a quick Google search, I located the names of a few funeral homes who charged reasonable rates and gave her their numbers.

"Thanks, Dez. I don't know what I would have done without your help."

"Call me back when you have the date for the service."

BY WEDNESDAY EVENING I was in the vestibule of Peaceful Transitions Funeral Home with about fifty of Susie's and Libby's closest friends. People spoke in hushed tones as they moved in and out of small groups, meeting and greeting each other. After a short time, the funeral director invited everyone into a compact room filled with rows of folding chairs with cushioned seats. Boxes of tissues sat on the floor near the middle of each row. Susie sat at the front wearing a black pantsuit with a vibrant blue blouse. What little makeup remained on her face could no longer hide the sorrow beneath.

"Ladies and gentlemen, thank you for joining us in this celebration of life for Elizabeth "Libby" Walker."

People began taking their seats and settling down.

"Susie has asked that I invite anyone who would like to speak about Libby to feel free to come to the front and do so."

Slowly, people trickled to the podium to await their turn. Many knew Libby from school and spoke about her sense of humor or her artistic ability. Apparently, she'd received an art scholarship to UNO. One person, a former boyfriend, talked about the time they zip lined and how scared he was, but that Libby made him laugh the entire time.

When it appeared that no one else remained, Susie stood sobbing, and ran from the room. A few women followed her out. I returned to the vestibule and waited for others to clear out of the ladies' room before going in to speak with Susie.

I found her sitting doubled over on a small couch in the restroom and sat next to her. Placing my arm around her shoulder, I handed her a box of tissues with the other.

"This sucks. That's all that can be said. It will feel like this for a while, but then, and I promise you this, it won't."

She looked up, tears streaming down her face.

"He did this."

"What?"

"That man. Castle. Rick Castle killed my sister."

"Susie, you don't know that. It's been ruled a suicide because there's no other evidence indicating anything different."

"No! They're wrong and I know they are. I can prove it." She reached into her jacket pocket and handed me a note.

"She left me this note asking me to pick up some crackers because she felt nauseous. That was Thursday morning. Why would she do that if she planned to kill herself?"

That was a good question, and I didn't have an answer.

"I don't know how he did it, but he did."

"Did you show the note to the police?"

"Yes, but they said it didn't prove anything. They said depressed people sometimes do things like this." She wiped her face with a tissue and then went to the sink. Wetting a paper towel, she applied it to her eyes, then face, and neck. "Please help me, Dez."

"What do you expect me to do?"

"She didn't commit suicide. I just need to know the truth."

"And what if that is the truth?"

She shook her head. "It's not."

"Susie, it could be and you're going to have to deal with that possibility."

She inhaled and exhaled slowly.

"I know he did something to Libby. I just need you to figure out what it was. Will you help me?"

There's no doubt that I have a soft spot for two things: cold cases and people who've been screwed over by someone who supposedly loved them. I end up taking my share of pro bono cases because of the latter.

FORTY-YEAR-OLD MEN messing with naïve nineteen-year-olds just pisses me off. What the hell can they possibly have in common? I can't speak for the women, but for the men it's about two things: sex and control. Getting emotionally involved in my cases is a something I generally avoid, but this one touched a nerve.

I'd left Susie inside the funeral home so I could organize my next moves. Jury duty set me behind on the Kincade case and I needed to get back to it, so I planned to have Clive dig up whatever he could about Rick Castle. All Susie could tell me was that he's some kind of researcher, but she had no clue what kind of research he did. Hopefully, nothing involving spiders or other creepy crawly things. Five minutes hadn't passed, and I was already thinking of this as my case. From the confines of my Jeep, I called Clive.

"Where are you?" I could hear banging in the background.

"Oh, um, hang on a minute."

The sound got muffled, so I couldn't quite make out what Clive was saying or who he was speaking to.

"Clive? I don't have all day."

"Yeah, yeah, sorry about that Ms. D."

"What are you doing?"

"I'm at Detrick's warehouse."

"Why?"

"He still has me listed as the contact for the utility companies. They needed to get inside for something with the meter."

"What was all that banging?" The minute I said the words aloud I realized that in the back of my mind I was entertaining the idea of buying the building. Why else would I give a shit about anything happening inside it? Damn it, Clive for putting the thought in my head in the first place.

"Some kids from my old high school needed a place to build their float for some parade they're doing."

Ah, Clive, always one to help everyone else — for a price.

"How much are you charging them?"

"What? Nah, it ain't like that."

"Really?"

"I know them real good, so I said they could use the space for a week or two."

"That's mighty nice of ya, Clive."

"Since you're paying me and I'm working at Eddy's, I don't need a whole lot now. Besides, it's important to give back to the community."

"Sure, it is. Listen, I need you to get background on a man named Rick Castle."

"Who is he?"

"That's what you need to tell me. All I know is that he does research and apparently might frequent certain UNO events."

"Time frame?"

"We'll touch base tomorrow morning at Do Space. I'm headed over to Kincade's store off Maple."

"You got it, Ms. D. I'm on it!"

IT WAS ALMOST TIME for the shift change at the Maple location, and I needed every light to be green for me to make it there, or I'd miss one employee I needed to get eyes on. The Irish was strong with me today; I made it with a few minutes to spare and pulled into a spot near an air hose. From there I could see whoever came and went. A guy named Micah was supposed to be heading out while another guy named Demi was coming in. Tonya might still be there, too. Her shift ended at three-thirty, but since I'd already reached out to her, she wasn't my priority.

As I pretended to get something from the back of my Jeep, I lingered long enough to see three employees inside the store, all chit-chatting. Customers lined up at the pumps, but none had entered the store and I couldn't see if there were any shopping. It seemed like the crew had nothing to do, which made little sense at this time of day. Then I remembered that this spot was closed recently for a few months to do some repair work to the pumps and had only reopened about two months ago. Customers had plenty of other choices in the area, so Kincade probably lost some business.

Since I didn't know who was who, I headed inside for a closer look. The chime of the bell as I entered stopped their conversation long enough for the one behind the counter to greet me with an abbreviates hello. The other two gave me a slight head nod. I pretended to look over a display rack of various chips across from the register, and their conversation appeared to pick up wherever I'd interrupted it.

"Man, that game last night was lit." The employee behind the counter spoke up.

"Shit, I lost 'bout three Benjamins."

"Always losing. You ever stop to think that maybe gambling ain't your strength?"

"Nah, coach, Lady Luck just hasn't been on my side lately, but things is turning 'round soon. I can feel it."

"Like last night?" Coach said. The guy behind the counter laughed.

I turned around, bag of chips in hand, looking like I had a question, and waited for them to notice. This provided ample opportunity for me to determine that 'coach' was a guy named Russell and the other guy was Micah. So that meant Demi was behind the counter.

"Do you need something?" Demi asked.

"Yeah, how much are these chips?"

"Sign says, 'buck fifty.'"

I made a show of looking back at the display rack and not being able to find the sign.

"It's right there." Micah pointed at a small sign at the top of the rack that Sherlock Holmes wouldn't have been able to see.

"Kind of small, isn't it?" I asked.

"Yeah, well, that's what The Man wants, I guess."

"The Man?"

"The owner. His cheap ass never wants to pay for nothing," Demi said.

"He wouldn't have paid to fix them pumps if he hadn't got caught," Russell said gesturing outside.

"Who you talkin' 'bout?" A women's voice cut into the conversation. "Kincade? Don't you know better than to bite the hand that feeds you? Talkin' shit to a cus," Then she saw me. "You got that application?"

The other three looked at her, back to me, and waited for my answer.

"I was over by his store in Benson, so I dropped it there. The lady said that would be okay."

"Lady? You mean Latrice?" Russell asked.

I shrugged.

"That bitch is always up in everybody's business." Demi said. "Thinks just because she's been working for Kincade the longest that she's special. He'd fire her ass without thinking twice if she wasn't giving him what he wants."

"Don't be startin' rumors, Demi," Tonya said.

"You know it's true," Micah said.

"I don't know nothing about it and neither do any of your narrow behinds," she said as she made her way to the exit. "Micah, you giving me a ride or not? I've got to get somewhere by four o'clock, remember?"

"Later," Micah said to Demi and Russell.

"You applied for a job here, huh?" Russell asked. "You're sure making an interesting life choice." He reached past me to grab a bag of Doritos. His bicep was slightly bigger than my thigh. "Put these on my tab," he told Demi, and then left the store.

"He's right. The only reason most of us work here is because he's not open twenty-four seven, so we don't have to work crazy-ass hours like those dumbasses at other stores. That, and he's usually not around much. We can sort of be our own boss."

"How long have you been working here?"

"I been here about a year, so I know Kincade better than most, except Latrice, of course. Micah and Russell got hired after me, and it looks like you already know Tonya."

"How much does he pay?"

"Minimum wage is where he says everybody starts, but my pay hasn't changed since I been here. I'm looking at making a change, though. Might take up a trade or something. I'm looking at classes at Metro."

I set the chips back onto the rack.

"Changed your mind?"

"Yeah, don't want to ruin my dinner. Thanks for the tips. Maybe I won't see you next time." I waved and smiled as I left.

Back inside my Jeep, I checked the time. Somehow, I'd been at Kincade's for nearly an hour. I really should have grabbed a few things to put into my car cooler since my next stop was to return to the Ida station. Instead, I opted to hit a Jimmy John's drive-thru for a club sandwich, a bag of chips, and a Coke. And maybe a cookie. Who am I kidding? I was definitely getting a cookie.

Jimmy John's is all about lightning-fast service. I don't know about any other fast-food joints, but I swear their drive-thru turnaround time has got to be one minute or less. They also never screw up my order, which isn't something I can say about any other place.

The window slid open; I handed the crew member my debit card, and he gave me my Coke, followed by a bag of delicious goodness. It's the bread. All the sandwiches are the same size and come encased in a soft French-style baguette. Or maybe it's Italian. It doesn't matter, I'd eat it either way. I set the bag onto the passenger seat and the coke in a drink holder before speeding away to Kincade's on Ida.

Chapter Five

AN EMPLOYEE NAMED MONIQUE was working the three-thirty to eight-thirty shift, and then Tate would be in after that. I planned to hang out for a while so I parked across the street, positioned so that I could see everyone who came and went. Monique seemed to know every customer who entered, which meant they were regulars, and this was probably the shift she worked most often.

A few white teenagers entered the store. One approached the counter and paid for whatever they'd picked up — something small from what I could tell — probably gum or mints. The other two wound their way through the aisles before returning to the front to pay for their handful of snacks. Monique didn't appear to know them. There wasn't the same level of interaction and chattiness that she'd done with several previous customers. The teens left just as a young black teen entered. Monique smiled but was more watchful than she had been with the others. Before she'd been reading a book, but this time she kept tabs on the kid. He found whatever he was looking for, paid, and left.

It was ten after eight and I wanted to check in with Monique before she left for the night. Since the Coke and bottle of water I'd had stashed in my cooler got me wiggling, now was an excellent time to do that. As I entered, I saw that she was cleaning the counter.

"Rest room?"

She looked up and pointed toward the back of the store.

A few minutes later when I returned to the front, I didn't see her, so I pretended to busy myself by looking through a magazine. I heard the click, click of her heels, and replaced the magazine in its spot.

"Hey, could I get an application?" I asked, walking toward her. She'd perched herself on a stool behind the counter. A pile of textbooks, that I assumed were hers, rested to one side of the register.

"Calculus, huh? That's a tough subject."

"Not to me." She handed me the application. "You can fill it out here or take it home and bring it back."

"Do you know if they have any openings at this store?"

"They might. One girl hasn't been showing up lately. Word is she's pregnant."

"Have you worked here long?"

"Long enough." She took the stack of books and placed them into a backpack.

"What do you think of the place?"

"Look, it's a convenience store that sells gas. What the hell would anybody think of it? It's a J-O-B. I have two others."

"What about the owner? He good to work for?"

"Please, I don't have time to worry about whether he's this way, or that way. I've got school and bills to pay. As long as he pays me in full and on time, I don't care what he does."

Fair enough. It was obvious I would not get much further with this line of questioning.

"I'll just fill this out over there," I said, pointed to a set of tables to the left of the entrance.

I took my time, not really filling it out because this would give me a better look at Tate when he arrived. Then, I could go back out, park my car on the street, sit back, and watch. I don't know what that conversation the other day was about between him and the other guy, but since I knew they worked together, and something wasn't quite right, monitoring at least one of them seemed prudent.

At eight-forty-five, Monique started pacing behind the counter and looking at a giant Go Big Red clock on the wall above the coolers. When she started talking to herself, I got a little concerned.

"I swear to God if he makes me late for my class, I'm gonna beat his ass." There was more pacing, followed by an F-bomb. "Where the hell is he?" Her eyes searched the front windows, darting from one section to the next.

At nine o'clock, Tate strolled into the store. Monique didn't say a word, just grabbed her backpack, walked past him, and punched his shoulder on her way out the door. The force was hard enough to knock him off balance, causing him to fall into the counter.

"Sorry, Monique!"

Tate wore faded jeans, a loose-fitting hoody, and purple Converse shoes. As he righted himself, he smoothed out the front of his hoody.

"I guess she's a little upset," he said looking at me.

"Maybe a little."

I folded the application and stood to leave, but decided a Snickers was a good idea. After giving Tate the money and tossing the application into a garbage can, I left the store. Tate didn't strike me as a person with much situational awareness, so I toyed with not moving my Jeep, but there was the off chance that I misjudged him; Just in case, I moved to the spot I'd been in when I first arrived.

More people filled their gas tanks than entered the store over the next few hours. I needed something to keep me awake and was thankful I'd purchased the Snickers. Around ten o'clock, I saw a familiar face. Randy, the guy from the other day drove up in a beat-up Chevy — model unknown mostly because I'm not much into old cars. I made a note of the plate.

When he entered the store, Tate picked up a bag from behind the counter and handed it to him. Randy opened it, grinned at Tate, and then closed the bag. They did a fist-bump before Randy returned to his car. The engine roared to life. As he pulled out of the lot, I turned my engine over and followed him.

WE DROVE A FEW MILES further north, eventually ending up in the lot of an older apartment complex called Shady Palm. Nothing about the building stood out. Each unit looked like the next. Overgrown bushes lined the parameter of each building, and the grass was several inches high compared to the sidewalks. Randy parked, while I found a spot a few cars back and away from him. Based on the outside appearance, I was guessing security wasn't all that tight. He led me to a building labeled with an 'A' and I took a quick picture, so I'd remember it later. When he entered the first set of doors, I waited for him to go in before following. Then I did what has never failed me, yet. I pushed buttons until someone let me inside.

Randy had taken the stairs, so I was betting he only went to the second floor. I hoofed it two stairs at a time and saw him enter an apartment at the end of the hall with the bag in his hands. I walked down the hall to get the apartment number, lingering outside it to eavesdrop. After a few minutes when I couldn't make anything out, I decided the effort was futile and went back to my Jeep.

At one o'clock in the morning, Randy exited the apartment building without the bag. He hopped into his car, turned it on, and sped out of the lot. I didn't see any point in following him this time, but I was curious about the contents of that bag. The only way I would discover that was to figure out who lived in apartment 210.

Chapter Six

AT SEVEN O'CLOCK IN the morning, the alarm on my phone blared. My heart raced as my hands fumbled to find it on the nightstand. I missed it and the damn thing crashed to the floor.

"Shit!"

I rolled over onto my stomach, extending my arm over the side of the bed, trying to grasp hold of it, my fingers barely reaching its smooth surface. It kept sliding and scooting until it disappeared just outside my reach, beneath the bed. From outside my bedroom door, I could hear Godfrey whining to go out.

"In a minute, Godfrey."

Acknowledging him increased the volume and insistence of his whining. Annoyed with both the alarm and Godfrey, I kicked my legs over the side of the bed, sat up, rolled my shoulders a few times, and got up. I'd gotten to bed late and was feeling it. The older I got, the worse it was. The days when I could pull an all-nighter and continue with the next day like it was nothing were becoming a distant memory. Now, I felt groggy, usually had a headache, and would rip a priest a new asshole if he so much as said, "Good morning."

I retrieved my phone from its hiding spot and did a quick scan for text messages. Thankfully, there were none. I'd fallen asleep in my clothes on the couch and eventually wandered upstairs, too tired to bother taking them off. My curls were probably flattened since I also didn't wrap my hair. I shuffled to the bathroom, confirming the status of my curls as I passed the mirror to start the shower.

The morning temperature was cooler than usual, so washing my hair was not on the agenda this morning. It would take too long for it to dry, and I had to meet Clive at Do Space at eight-thirty. I gathered my hair into a shower cap and eased into the shower. The heated water falling on my body was like a hug you never wanted to end. It lulled me into a more relaxed state, and I longed to return to bed smothered in my down blanket. Then, my father's booming voice cut through. "Snap out of it, Jackson! You've got shit to do today."

I turned the shower knob to cold, and the blast jarred me from my reverie. Nothing makes me move faster than my dad barking orders, and icy water streaming down my body. It works every time I need a kick in the ass to get my day going.

Today's wardrobe wasn't any different from yesterday, except cleaner. I started with a pair of bootcut jeans, followed by a V-neck, long-sleeved T-shirt, and black motorcycle boots. I hooked the clasp of my gold shamrock necklace and it fell to just above my breastbone. My sister Savannah gave me the necklace for my thirteenth birthday not long before she was murdered. I paired it with small hoop earrings. My curls fell out of the cap to my shoulders. Now that I was more alert, they didn't look as flat as I thought. I spritzed them with water, did a little rearranging, and then left them alone. You don't mess with the curls once they're in place. Frizz is not your friend. Besides, everyone knows you don't touch a Black woman's hair, or even a biracial woman's hair. That's simply a "no-no."

Godfrey had apparently given up getting me to open the door because his whining had stopped. My guess was that I'd find him slumped in a heap outside my door, ready to give me 'the guilt eyes' for ignoring him. I opened the door, and he didn't move. Yep, he was upset.

Moving a hundred- and thirty-pound pouting Rottweiler isn't easy, and I don't advise ever trying to do it. The best course of action is to offer a treat as a peace offering. Stepping over his body, I descended the stairs and went directly to the kitchen. There was no pitter-patter of his paws behind me, so I knew this was serious. He never liked being ignored and locked out my bedroom.

By the time I opened and closed the refrigerator door, Godfrey sat behind me, staring up expectantly.

"Enough with the pouting, Godfrey. Here." I handed him a generously sized piece of left-over steak. He gobbled it in one bite, then stared at me, his head tilted slightly to the left.

I sighed. "Fine." There was more steak in the fridge. People might not have ESP, but I would bet a Benjamin that dogs do. I gave him the rest and grabbed a bottle of OJ for myself.

"That's all, Godfrey."

He walked to the door and waited for me to let him out.

"You know what would be great?" He looked up at me, and I knew he understood everything I said. Yeah, I know, dog owners always say that, but it's because dogs have eyebrows and do the head tilting thing when you talk to them. If that doesn't mean they understand, then what does it mean? Cats don't do that. I hate cats.

After letting him out and filling his water dish, I made myself a light breakfast. A nearly burned Everything bagel with cream cheese goes perfectly with Breakfast Serenade tea from The Tea Trove. The aroma of the blend is intoxicating, and just enough of a pick-me-up that I've kicked my Coke with breakfast habit.

Checking the wall-mounted clock, it was already eight-fifteen. I needed to high tail it out to get to Do Space on time. Being late for appointments is not only unprofessional, but disrespectful. I avoid it whenever possible, and it's one thing Clive still needs to learn. I grabbed my jacket and satchel on the way out, leaving the dirty dishes for later.

CLIVE WAS IN HIS USUAL spot, clicking away on the keyboard of the Mac I'd purchased to replace the old laptop he was using. He wore a turned back ball cap, faded jeans and a black T-shirt with an image of Tupac in a business suit. Beneath the image, it read, 'trust nobody.'

He looked up from the computer when I dropped my satchel onto the table.

"Morning, Ms. D. I think I got exactly what you wanted to know about this Castle dude."

"Shoot," I said, and sat across from him.

"Castle is forty-three years old, been married for twenty years to Patricia Allen-Castle. They've got two kids, both teenagers. Daughter goes to Marian and son goes to Prep. His research is crazy scary."

"What do you mean?"

"He figures out how to use music to torture people. Not just that, though. The dude studies how it can be used during interrogations. It got me thinking about the times I got picked up. They never used music that I recall."

"Anything else?"

"Yeah, a shitload. It turns out there's more out there about it 'cause it was used at Guantánamo and Abu Ghraib. You ever heard of The Mosquito?"

I shook my head.

"You probably wouldn't hear it, anyway. It's a device that uses a high frequency sound to make people my age go 'poof.'" He gestured with his hands like he was a magician doing a disappearing card trick.

"I'm not that old, Clive."

"I know, I'm just saying that this device targets people under twenty-five, so you'd be safe. I heard it on a YouTube video, and it made my head split."

"So, Castle studies sound and how to hurt people?"

"Yeah. The dude's whack."

"Great. This should be interesting. I assume you have his contact information."

Clive grabbed his phone, his thumbs moving in a flurry only possible by a Gen-Z youth. My phone vibrated.

"There you go. Text and email, just in case."

I stood to leave. "One more thing, I need you to get me pictures of these two guys." I handed a notecard with Tate's and Randy's personal details. "When you get the pictures, email or text them to me. Then, see what you can find out about a woman who lives at this address." I handed him a second notecard.

"Will do, Ms. D. I'm on it!"

I returned to my Jeep and called Castle's place of employment to make an appointment. In most situations like this, where I need to get information from someone who might be reluctant to provide it, I lie. During my first years with Tracer International, I could never look someone straight in the face, lie, and be convincing. Now it was second nature.

As far as Castle's secretary was concerned, I was a freelance journalist writing a story for a scientific journal. It's one of my favorite go-to covers. She informed me that Mr. Castle had a tight schedule, but she could squeeze me in Monday afternoon for fifteen minutes. My appointment set, I was ready to move on to my next task — training at Simmons Martial Arts Academy.

BY THE TIME I FINISHED my workout and got cleaned up, I had several messages from Clive. He'd sent the pictures of Tate and Randy and had the information about the woman in apartment 210, including a picture. Way to go, Clive. Her name was Chrystal Moyer, and she worked at a nursing home close to Shady Palms Apartments, called Beautiful Day. According to what Clive found, Chrystal was twenty-three years old, had two kids, both in foster care, and a few arrests for solicitation and drugs, but no convictions.

I called Beautiful Day to see if I could get a fix on Chrystal's schedule. The very helpful receptionist informed me that Chrystal was unavailable, but her current shift ended at one o'clock. She was just working part time in housekeeping and was not usually still there at this time of day, but had agreed to cover for someone who was a no show in the kitchen. By all accounts, Chrystal was a wonderful young lady who was always willing to lend a hand. The receptionist invited me to leave a message; I opted not to. Instead, I drove over to Beautiful Day and waited for Chrystal to leave.

On my way there, I pulled through Jimmy John's drive-thru, ordered a number six with Thinny chips, a Coke, and water. I had a little time to kill before I expected her to leave the home, so I figured I'd eat lunch in their parking lot and catch up on emails.

I receive a dizzying amount of crap email, mostly because I don't configure my spam filters. At some point, I will break down and ask Haithem if his assistant Dalton can take care of it for me, but for now I just hit delete.

Haithem Nazari is a former colleague and mentor from my days working at Tracer International. I got recruited from college and he was part of my last test in their program. Tracer puts candidates through rigorous tactical and psychological training. Most people fail. The last test typically involves a high-profile case, but one that they've manipulated in some way. Team sizes vary based on the number of remaining candidates, and members don't always play nicely with each other. Tracer intentionally matches people who've clashed throughout training up to that point. The teams submit a logistical plan and pass or fail based on its execution. Mine involved a stolen diamond and expensive artwork. Haithem played the role of the evildoer in disguise.

Since leaving Tracer we've stayed connected, and I stepped into his position on a while a few months ago, while he was helping me with a case that finally solved my sister's murder. Haithem is a senior analyst with an elite team of researchers and hackers at his disposal. He's intelligent, fit, and has an accent that will make your panties drop.

His assistant Dalton and I got better acquainted when I took over for Haithem. He always seemed to know when I was entering the building in Lincoln and would greet me. It didn't matter if I rode the elevator, or took the stairs, there he was, reports in hand, ready for me. I checked my satchel and jacket for a tracking device, but never found one.

Even though he's Haithem's assistant, he also can find any information you want, and a bunch you don't, on almost anyone in the US, and in several other countries. Tracer started recruiting him in high school, which is rare, but he's never been in the field. Dalton is strictly back-office material.

I sent Haithem an email just checking in, so that when I hit him up for Dalton's help it wouldn't be entirely out of the blue. Then I continued my deletion project.

At five minutes after one, Chrystal walked out of Beautiful Day, and got into an old silver Chevy pickup. I followed her out of the lot, and through the neighborhood until we reached 72nd Street. She traveled south to a mall area, parked, and entered a convenience store. I waited. A few minutes later she returned with a pack of cigarettes, opened it, and lit up before getting back inside her truck. From there, she drove back to Shady Palms Apartments.

After she entered the building, I gave her about five minutes to get settled, then followed her. I didn't need to use my button-pressing trick because someone was coming out as I went in. This time I took the elevator. My legs were already getting sore from my workout earlier. She didn't answer on the first knock, so I tapped on the door a little harder.

She opened the door wearing a yellow t-shirt, pajama bottoms, and bunny slippers. I introduced myself and gave her my card.

"What's this about?"

"Do you mind if I come in for a minute?"

"Knock yourself out." She opened the door, allowing me to pass her. "I was just getting something to drink. Do you want anything?"

"No, thank you. I'm good."

She returned from the kitchen with a glass of water. I pulled up the picture of Randy James first and showed it to her.

"Do you happen to know this man?"

"No, can't say that I do. Should I?"

I pulled up the next one of Tate Hill.

"How about this one?"

She shook her. "Sorry, they don't look familiar."

"Oh, are you sure?"

She made a show of looking at both pictures again more intently, then shook her head.

"Sorry for wasting your time." I moved toward the door.

"Did they do something wrong? Why are you lookin' for them?"

"You don't need to worry about them. I'm just doing a few preliminary background checks for my client. They're planning to reward a few employees and are trying to determine the best fit. That's all."

"Why ask me?"

"Randy James and Tate Hill both lived in this complex not so long ago. I'm just trying to reach out to people who might have interacted with them. You know, to get a feel for their situations. Thanks again for your time." I opened the door to leave.

"Should I tell them you came by?"

I turned back. "I thought you didn't know them?"

She looked at her feet, then back up at me.

"I didn't want to get them into any kind of trouble, but you said this is for a reward, so,"

"How long have you known them?"

"A few years. We went to high school together. They're really nice."

A bag on a kitchen chair caught my attention.

"Have they ever gotten into any trouble?"

"Just the usual kinds of stuff. Speeding, smoking weed, that sort of thing. Nothing real bad or anything. They're like brothers, you know?"

"Real or like 'brothers from another mother?'"

"They're stepbrothers, but always got along real good, so they shared an apartment here, just down the hall from me."

"You a student?"

"Huh? Hmm, no, why?"

"I was just noticing the backpack, that's all."

"Oh, yeah, um, that's just some baby stuff. Money's been tight and Randy brought me a few things."

"Where are your kids?"

"Foster, but I get to see them, you know, with supervision."

"You've been very helpful."

"So, should I tell them or is this a secret?"

"It's a secret. Thanks."

I LEFT CHRYSTAL MOYER'S place feeling a little disappointed. I was hoping that this Kincade case would wrap up quickly. Tate and Randy looked like viable suspects, but Moyer's depiction of them made them out to be good Samaritans. Still, I wasn't sure I completely bought that story, but until something else popped, there wasn't any reason to keep going down that path.

The longer I sat around in my Jeep, the tighter my leg muscles got, so I decided to go home and get caught up on paperwork. One thing I didn't have Clive doing yet was invoicing clients. I like to keep a close eye on my money. When my aunt Violet left me the house, I was in decent shape financially, but it's always good practice to keep an eye toward the horizon.

Whenever I feel like my day-to-day finances are getting pinched, I hit Haithem up for a side job. He's always got something that needs a fresh pair of experienced eyes on it. I left Tracer on good terms and might have stayed longer if they hadn't stuck me in Miami for an eternity. That place was sucking my compassionate nature dry. I had to get out before that happened. Some might think New York City was a strange choice after Miami, but my family are east coast people. We were military, but the east coast was home, and every other place was a pit stop, including Omaha. The only reason I returned is because passing up a free house and a lower cost of living seemed prudent.

I arrived home, checked the mailbox — no bills — and went inside, setting my satchel onto a chair in my office and tossing my jacket over the back of the couch as I passed. Godfrey's paws scratched at the back door. When I didn't respond as quickly as he'd like, he barked.

Godfrey was five years old when I adopted him. I don't know what made me do it, but I suspect it was the way his droopy eyes looked up at me when I walked through the kennel area at the pound. All the other dogs barked, and some growled, but Godfrey was quiet. When I approached his kennel, his massive head titled to the left like he was sizing me up. All the kennels have signs describing the dog, including things like how trainable they are, and what they like. He only had his name and story because he was a relatively recent arrival. I called his name, but he didn't so much as flinch. When I gave him a command, though, he raised his large, muscular body from the cot, and came to the kennel door. I told him to sit, and he did. I knew then he was my kind of dog. He could take you or leave you until you proved that you deserved his attention.

I let Godfrey inside, and he followed me back to my office. For the rest of the afternoon I sorted, documented, and created invoices for cases. I caught up on past due invoices, calling each one to remind them. Chasing my money was my least favorite part of the job. People are excited to get you involved and solving their problems, but when you do, they're slow to pay. Of course, it's not everyone, but it only takes a few to make a smart PI understand that a percent of payment upfront is non-negotiable. At least that way you're not completely screwed.

Around five-thirty I cleared my desk, stood, and stretched. Every muscle in my back hurt, and I'd been sitting so long, my legs cramped. After a few touch-my-toes moves, things started loosening up again, but I knew I'd need an ibuprofen. I slid open my top desk drawer, grabbed and opened the bottle, then popped one into my mouth, swallowing it without water. Godfrey followed me back to the kitchen, his feet doing a little happy dance when he realized I was getting 'the good food' for him. Usually I fed him dry food, but once or twice each week I surprised him with canned.

Since cooking dinner was rarely on my agenda, I ordered Thai takeout, and eagerly awaited its arrival. When it came, I tipped the driver five bucks, and then plopped on the couch for dinner and a movie. When the movie was over, my mind wandered and landed on my meeting with Rick Castle tomorrow afternoon. I'd never heard much about his type of research, and it made me curious what kind of person studies manipulation and torture.

At ten-thirty I crawled beneath my down comforter, but sleep was elusive. I didn't know what was keeping me awake, but suspected it was images from the movie. I probably shouldn't have watched The Shining. My cell phone told me it was two a.m. If I got up now, I'd be worthless by the time I met with Castle. Counting backwards from one hundred, I slowly relaxed. The next time I awoke it was to the annoying screech of my cell phone, and the bot voice telling me it was seven o'clock.

Chapter Seven

TRAFFIC AT EIGHT-THIRTY in the morning on a weekday in Omaha isn't too difficult to navigate. A lot of people head east to downtown, so I just avoid that until they're safely nestled inside their offices, off the streets, and out of my way. Students are already at school, so getting stuck behind busses isn't a problem either.

This morning I planned to give Kincade an update, so he knew he was getting his money's worth. When I entered the Benson location, Latrice was working, again. While she assisted a customer, I hung out by the magazines leafing through the latest copy of Guns & Ammo. I'm not a fan of guns, but they're a necessary part of the job. Mostly I like anything stick-like — staff, quarter staff, canes, pointy umbrellas — things you don't need a permit to carry, but that can do enough damage to stop someone in their tracks. Not everyone needs a bullet in their body to keep them down. But some people aren't as comfortable with hand-to-hand combat as I am, so I understand why they'd pick a weapon that can cause permanent, and irreversible damage from a distance. I just wish it was harder for dumbasses to get them.

"Good morning, Ms. Jackson."

"Hi, Latrice. Is Tom in the office?"

"Yep. He's in a foul mood, though."

"Why?"

"More inventory came up missing."

"Thanks for the heads up."

I walked back to Kincade's office mentally prepared for an attack. The door was open, and Kincade sat behind his desk scrutinizing stacks of inventory lists. I knocked on the door.

"Jackson! What the hell is going on? I hired you to take care of this." He tossed a handful of papers toward me. They landed near the edge of the desk, and I left them there.

"These things take time."

"Swan would have had this handled yesterday."

"Maybe, but he's unavailable, so if you still want my services, you're going to need to be patient." Still standing in the doorway, I removed a notebook from my satchel. "What do you know about Tate and Randy?"

"Why? Is it them?"

"I'm just following up on a conversation I had with someone who knows them."

"They're young, stupid, and think with their cocks. What else do you need to know?"

"Why'd you hire them?"

"Please. Do you have any idea how hard it is to hire anybody at minimum wage? Christ, I'm lucky I'm not stuck with released convicts as my only option. It's bad enough I've got all these Colored people."

A chill started beneath my hairline and continued straight down my back. I adjusted my stance and reminded myself not to bitch-slap my client.

"When did you hire them?"

"A few months back, I don't remember. Latrice could tell you. They both graduated from Northwest."

"What kind of employees are they? Do you ever have to get after them?"

"Tate has trouble telling time. Randy's never late. But if they're together, they're always late. I had them help with a few side jobs during the summer. Shit-for-brains, but then, that's pretty much every teenage boy around here."

"Any girlfriends?"

"Why the fuck would I care about that?"

"Have you seen them go out of their way to be helpful?"

He pushed his chair back and leaned with his hands clasped behind his head.

"You really are worthless. Why Swan recommended you,"

"Mr. Kincade, I'm trying to verify information from another source, so your perspective about your staff is important. I get the impression from most of them that you're a 'hands off' kind of boss unless something negatively affects your pocket. That leaves your employees free to do virtually whatever they want. Some mentioned that you spend most of your time at this location. I noticed that you have cameras installed in all your stores. I'll need to see that footage. As for Tate and Randy, at this point I don't believe they're responsible, but of course, I want to be sure before moving on to other possibilities. So, would you generally characterize them as helpful?"

"Yeah, I guess so."

"How did they get along with other team members?"

"Fine, except with Monique."

"Do you have the video surveillance footage for the past few months?

"It only goes back fourteen days."

He got the cheapest plan he could find. Perfect.

"That should be good since Latrice told me you just discovered more items missing. I'm assuming that happened in the past week to fourteen days?"

He nodded.

"Okay, then point me in the direction of your system and let's see what we can find out."

"You don't think I already did that? There's nothing to see."

"Maybe, but I should take a look just in case."

He turned to the computer behind his desk, tapped a few keys, and brought up the footage.

"Knock yourself out. I'll be right back."

I had to move into the hallway to let him out of the small office. After he was out of sight, I took his seat. The only store footage he pulled up was for Ida and Maple. I reviewed both. All the employees know exactly where every camera is in and around the stores, but like most people they forget they're being watched. I saw people picking their noses, filling their cups from the soda machine, smoking weed, and making out with someone during or after a late shift. Once in a while, Tate or Randy would look directly at a camera and give it the finger with a big smile.

Finding nothing useful, I pulled up the file for the Benson location. Latrice worked almost every day. There were three other employees during the fourteen days of footage. Kincade hadn't asked me to investigate any of them. His assumption was that they didn't know employees from the other stores and that whoever was stealing was doing it alone. I had other ideas. Most of his staff didn't like him and I could see one or two, maybe even three of them conspiring to steal merchandise to sell later. The question was still who, but I was narrowing the field.

"You finished?" His gruff voice interrupted my thoughts.

I stood, came around the desk, and exited the room allowing him to enter.

"Nothing, right? I told ya."

"I wouldn't say that," I said and turned to leave. "I'll be back in touch when I have something solid."

On my way out, I noticed Latrice restocking a shelf of candy bars and pre-packaged cookies. She was setting aside some, but not others.

"Doing a little sorting?"

"Yeah, I put the new ones in the back or underneath the older ones. If something's damaged, then I take it to the front and discount it."

"So, you still sell the damaged ones?"

"Sure, people always looking for a deal, you know?"

"What happens when they don't sell?"

"They usually do."

The notification on my phone vibrated and I checked the time. It was almost one o'clock and my appointment with Rick Castle was in thirty minutes. I reached around Latrice and grabbed a Hershey with almonds.

"Lunch?" She asked grinning.

"True sustenance."

She followed me to the register. Always a sucker for point-of-sale items, I snatched up a pack of gum, some Altoids, and a discounted bag of Cheetos. She was on point. People like deals.

RICK CASTLE WORKED for SMT Tech, a company who primarily handled military contracts. They produce a variety of advanced weapon systems. Most of what they do is create scary stuff that no American would ever want used against them, but are fine having used on prison populations, or against foreign threats. Growing up with a Marine for a father doesn't automatically mean I have to agree with everything the military does, but it does mean I have to respect the people expected to deploy actions on behalf of America. It's a fine line and has led to more than one heated discussion with my father.

The office, located in a rather nondescript industrial rehabbed building just south of downtown, was large enough to accommodate drones and tanks. I entered on the ground floor through a set of glass double doors. Someone in a lab coat stood about fifty feet from the entrance surrounded by several people in business suits. She gestured to various weapons protected in display cases, and drone prototypes that hung from the ceiling.

A man dressed in a black tactical uniform sat in command of the centrally located reception desk. When I approached, he greeted me politely, asked for identification, scanned it, and then gave me a badge.

"You'll need this to access the lower levels. When you get into the elevator, swipe this in front of the pad to your right, above the floor numbers. Before you leave, be sure to drop your badge into that bin." He pointed to a square receptacle near the edge of the desk.

I nodded, and he directed me to the elevators behind the desk and down a wide hallway. Several people, some in lab coats, and others in suits, emptied from the elevator before I stepped inside. I followed his instructions, the doors closed, and the elevator whooshed downward to the basement labs. They opened into a small waiting area. To the left, an older woman sat behind a desk listening intently to the person at the other end of the call. Behind her was a wall of glass treated with security film so that no one could see through it. I walked over and waited for her to acknowledge me. She finished her discussion and smiled.

"You're here to see Dr. Castle, correct?"

"Yes."

"He'll be out momentarily. Can I get you water, coffee, tea, or soda?"

"No, thank you."

"Please have a seat."

I opted to stand but moved closer to the seating area so that I didn't make the receptionist uncomfortable. A few tech-related magazines littered a coffee table, but none caught my attention enough to compel me to page through them. After a few minutes, the sliding doors opened, and a tall man, with greying hair and a goatee, walked toward me. His white lab coat hid what was obviously a lean, fit body.

Extending his hand, he said, "You must be Ms. Jackson. Welcome to my lab. We don't have much time for a full tour, but we'll do our best. Shall we?" He gestured to the doors. They slid quietly into place behind us as we entered.

"So, you're a freelance writer? That must be interesting work."

"Certainly not more interesting than what you're doing here."

He waved this off like it was nothing.

"We're just trying to make the world a safer place."

We continued walking through various sections of the lab with him pointing out aspects he thought would most interest my readers, but cautioned me saying, "Please no photos. I'm sure you can understand."

"I understand that you're working with ways to better weaponized sound and music. Tell me more about that."

"The overview is this, I'm sure you're familiar with a device called The Mosquito?"

I nodded. "It emits a sound that can only be heard by people under the age of twenty-five, if I recall correctly."

"Exactly. So, we're already able to control certain types of people using high or low frequencies. My lab is currently extending that work."

"I see. How are you using music?"

"I'm afraid I can't comment too extensively on that specifically, but if you research the use of music during wartime, then that will give you a wealth of information. For instance, were you aware that during World War II the Nazi's used polka music in the camps? The juxtaposition of the upbeat melody mixed with the tragedy of the circumstances was designed to further demoralize the already beaten down prisoners."

"I didn't realize that. I'm more familiar with its use by American soldiers. It's strange to me that it's not considered a form of psychological warfare."

"Luckily for us it's not." He smiled. "Some theorists believe that the purpose of music from ancient times until more recently was to instill fear and dread in one's enemies. From the steady beat of drums to the seemingly innocuous songs used by rebel slaves' music stirs the pot, so to speak."

"How did you get into this line of research?"

"I was a music major during my undergrad, then psychology caught my eye, specifically the intersection of music and social behavior, but soon I was drawn to what some might consider the dark side of social behavior." He glanced at his watch.

"I can understand using sound to control crowd behaviors, but how could it be used to control an individual?"

"If you wanted to manipulate a person's mental capacity, then I suppose it would be possible to use sound to do that, but that's not the exact direction of my research."

He looked at his watch, again more pointedly.

"I've kept you longer than I intended." I extended my hand. "Thank you for talking with me. May I contact you if I have any further questions?"

"Certainly. Of course, it would be my pleasure." He escorted me to the exit. The doors slid open, I stepped through, and they closed behind me.

RICK CASTLE'S WIFE Patricia taught communications classes at a local community college. According to what Clive dug up, I'd be able to find her there tonight. She happened to be giving a lecture about podcasting and it was open to the public. Clive mentioned that the talk covered the ins and outs of various platforms, hosting options, and equipment. He seemed genuinely interested and I considered sending him, but he wasn't ready to interview someone like Patricia Castle, yet.

I had a few hours to kill, so I stopped by Brazen Head for a pint and Boxty. The already filled parking lot forced me to park farther away from the pub than I wanted, but my craving for a Boxty couldn't be ignored. Music escaped the confines of the bar as a few patrons entered ahead of me. People occupied every table and nook. Several patrons, engaged in casual conversations, stood near the wraparound wooden bar. I saw Mick pouring a pint of Guinness. When I caught his eye, he nodded, grabbed another glass, and filled it. After delivering the first one to a guy seated at the far end of the bar, he brought mine to me. Squeezing behind a guy the size of a UNL linebacker, I pushed forward.

"Hello, Dez. How are you this evening?" Mick said, his words giving away his Dublin origins.

"Is this a larger than usual Happy Hour crowd, or am I just imagining that?"

"A bit, yeah. There's a band playing tonight. Special occasion for some fellas over there," he said, gesturing with a small, raised chin.

"Are you getting a bite to eat?"

"Yeah, a Boxty."

"If you swing around the other side, I think I can get you a spot."

He disappeared to the other side. My initial attempts to snake my way through the crowd failed. Tired of the "excuse me" dance, I simply said, "move." It came out harsher than I intended but was more effective. As promised, Mick had cleared and reserved a spot for me.

"Thanks," I said and tossed my leather jacket around the back of the chair.

"How are things with you and Cynthia?"

"Good, I think," he said, while grabbing a few glasses and filling them. Someone behind me had just ordered. He took their card and turned away to run it through the register. After returning it to the customer, Mick dashed to the other side of the bar.

Cynthia Cruz is an investigative journalist friend of mine. We became acquainted when she attended a self-defense seminar I gave at one of the local YMCAs. She approached me after the class asking about private lessons. I don't give them often, but someone was stalking her, so we scheduled a series of weekly lessons. I knew she would benefit from learning a few well-executed locks that I don't normally cover during a seminar. We still train a few times per week. From time-to-time, she helps me out with research and the occasional interview. Cynthia likes to dabble in PI work but isn't ready to jump ship and go full time. She and Mick have been an exclusive item for a few months.

A server set my Boxty on the bar in front of me, and I swear my heart skipped. It'd been a long time since I'd had a Boxty. My mother used to make it all the time. It's basically an Irish pancake, but that's oversimplifying its hearty goodness, and the warmth that surges through your body as you eat one. I savored every bite, intermingling it with a swallow or two of Guinness. When I finished, I pushed the plate forward and leaned against the back of my seat.

"Another round?"

"Not tonight, I've got somewhere else to be, and I need a somewhat clear head." He showed me the bill, and I handed him my card.

After saying my goodbyes and promising not to stay away so long — which only amounted to me not being in the pub during the week I had jury duty — I left. Broken bits of leaves, twigs, and gravel mixed with dirt swirled on the ground as I walked to my Jeep. I wasn't looking forward to winter and the frigid temperatures, or the fact that business slowed when it got cold outside. That was something I hadn't anticipated when I made the move back to Omaha.

The lecture was at Do Space and only five minutes away from Brazen Head, so I didn't need to rush. As I drove south toward Dodge Street, a traffic jam stretched at least five blocks ahead of me. An accident tied up several east bound lanes, and no one was letting anyone else move into the open lane. Fifteen minutes later, I sat in the same spot waiting for an opening. The welcome blare of police sirens assured me that there'd be progress soon. A member of OPD arrived and began diverting traffic and stopping eastbound drivers from inching forward to block cars from entering from cross streets. I crossed through to the other side to avoid the continued standstill. There was more than one way to get where I needed to be.

I arrived ten minutes late and was directed to the upper-level classrooms. As a rule, I'm rarely late. It's a pet-peeve I've had, probably because of growing up with a military father. If we were on time, we were late. What 'on time' meant to my father was 'be five minutes early.'

Entering the back of the room, I spotted an open seat and eased into it as quietly as possible. Patricia Castle had already started speaking. Her current slide showed images of the names of various platforms like Spreaker, Simplecast, and Blog Talk Radio. She explained the popularity of podcasting and how much it'd grown in recent years. Thirty minutes later she invited members of the audience to record a podcast. She'd prepped a table with microphones and a laptop. When no one came forward, she volunteered a few on her own. I slid down in my seat, hoping she wouldn't notice, and breathed a sigh of relief when she skipped me. Four lucky people sat around the table, unsure what to do next.

Patricia patiently guided them through the microphone set-up explaining to everyone how things connected. Her laptop screen projected on a wall so we could see what she used to record their conversation. It was software called Audacity that she assured us was free. The ragtag team of newly minted podcasters introduced themselves, and then she led them through an interview about why they were interested in podcasting, and what they might call their future shows. After another thirty minutes, she wrapped it all up, showed us a little editing through Audacity, and concluded with a plug for her classes through the community college.

A few people lingered to ask more questions, and I waited until they left so I could introduce myself. Patricia was about five feet seven inches tall, with dirty blonde, shoulder-length hair. Her slender frame gave me the impression that she didn't eat much, or maybe she just had a high metabolism.

"Mrs. Castle?"

She'd begun disconnecting the microphones and winding cords to put into a large, plastic wheeled case with a long handle.

"Call me Patricia, please." She looked up, smiling.

"My name is Dezeray Jackson and I'm writing an article about your husband and his work. I'd love to talk with you."

"I don't have anything to do with his work." She continued winding the cords and placing them into the case.

"I'd like to include details about the family who has supported his rise in the research world. The family is so often overlooked, don't you think?"

"Overlooked? That's an understatement."

"Do you have time now, or perhaps tomorrow?"

The vibration of her phone on the table interrupted us.

"Excuse me, one second. I have to take this."

She stepped away, speaking in hushed tones. Her shoulders tensed as she said, "I can't talk, now. I'll call you later. No, that won't be necessary."

She ended the call and returned to her task, closing the computer, and packing it away with the other equipment. An almost imperceptible shake overtook her body.

"Is everything okay?"

"Yes, yes, I'm fine, really. How about tomorrow morning around nine?"

"Do you want to meet here, or,"

"Here would be perfect. I'll meet you in the café downstairs."

ONE OF THE BEST THINGS about the arrival of fall is saying bye-bye to mowing every week or, in my case, pay someone to do it. I contemplated this as I put my Jeep into park in my driveway. Aunt Violet had maintained the house, including the landscaping, and was a master gardener without the official title. I struggled to keep her rosebushes, that lined a bed just outside the bay window, from turning into brown, pointy twigs. Plants that I didn't know the names of followed the cement pathway to the front steps, and I wasn't completely convinced they were just dormant due to the weather changing. I like the idea of gardening much more than the execution. To be honest, if my entire lawn was rocks, boulders, and artificial plants, I'd be perfectly fine with that.

Godfrey was in the backyard when I came into the house, and I could hear him scraping and whining at the door. After kicking off my boots and hanging up my jacket on a hook near the door, I noticed a note on the table from Murphy. In all our time together since he returned, he's never left a note longer than maybe a five-word sentence.

Dez, I know you hate when I disappear without a trace, but I want you to know I appreciate that you never push for explanations. Not sure when I'll be back, but I'll be in touch — this time.

Murphy

As much as it annoys me that he does a Houdini once in a while, I gotta say that I like my autonomy. I like not feeling obligated, but this was an interesting shift in his M.O. We never talk about our relationship or even define it as one. When he's gone, I keep doing my thing, and I assume he does whatever it is he does, with whoever he does it. It's not that I'm sleeping with every good-looking man that crosses my path, but I'm not saying 'no' all the time either. A girl's gotta have a little fun. This note might be his way of taking things to a different level, and I'm not sure I want to go there. I refolded the note, and set it back onto the table, surprised that Murphy wrote it.

Godfrey started barking because I still hadn't let him inside, and I was sure he was starving since I'd only given him a few cups of food this morning. Before letting him inside, I filled his food and water dish, then I slid the deck door open and stood out of the way. He barreled past me and made a beeline for his food. Less than thirty seconds later, it was gone, and he crashed onto his dog bed.

"That's about how I feel, Godfrey."

I made popcorn, filled a glass with Chardonnay, and went back to the living room to watch a show. After scrolling through Netflix, Prime, and Hulu, I finally settled on The Expanse. I'd finished season four, but now was binge-watching the first three seasons, again. Amos is funny as hell and the actor playing their pilot wanders into my dreams some nights. I'm not a big fan of James Holden — he can be a little too weepy for my tastes. Godfrey decided to join me and positioned himself on the floor between the couch and coffee table. I pulled a blanket over my feet, turned up the volume on the TV, and relaxed.

Chapter Eight

"PATRICIA, THANKS AGAIN for meeting with me," I said, taking the seat opposite hers. "Can I get you something to drink? Coffee, tea?"

"I've already had two cups. If I have any more, I won't sleep at all tonight. I'm really trying to cut back, but caffeine is my BFF."

"I'm a tea drinker, but once in a while a mocha isn't such a bad thing."

"I spoke with Rick just to be sure he'd be okay with us chatting."

"Oh, is there some reason he wouldn't be?"

"He wants to be sure I don't talk too specifically about his work, but then I reminded him I don't know many of the specifics because he doesn't share them, so this isn't a problem as far as I'm concerned."

Wow, that was a mouthful. I sensed some animosity worth investigating. Maybe the happy couple wasn't so happy after all. Maybe Patricia wasn't as naïve as her husband seemed to believe. In my experience, the cheating spouse is never as clever as they convince themselves that they are. Their partners almost always suspect something, which is why I get hired. Sure, they'd rather I prove them wrong and reveal the innocence of their lying spouse, but in the ten years I've worked as a private investigator, that's never happened. If you think someone is lying to you, you're probably right. It's because we all have tells, and it's usually more than one that's giving us away. They're subtle behaviors, but when we're backed into a corner, they leak like a tire with a nail stuck in it.

"How long have you two been together?"

"Married twenty years. We met during college and probably should have waited until after graduate school, but one thing led to another, and I was pregnant."

"You haven't always lived in Omaha."

"We spent a little time on the west coast because that's where Rick got his first post-doc work. That was followed by a move to the east coast, and then a short stint in the UK before coming to Omaha. We've been here a few years. It's not as lively as the other places, but it has its own charm."

"I read your school bio. Why limit yourself to teaching community college courses? I mean, a Ph.D. should be able to open a lot of doors in your field."

"Some, but Rick needed me to be more available. If I was tied to a position that would decrease the flexibility he needed so he could pursue the jobs that interested him. I was fine with that at the time because I was pregnant. Who was going to hire me full time in that condition, I mean realistically? Then, we got pregnant with our second child, and I was still nursing our first. It was exhausting. I stayed home until they both could get into preschool, then eased into a few teaching opportunities wherever we happened to be living. Sometimes, I did private tutoring or gave a small lecture series. Honestly, I ended up liking it more than I think I would have enjoyed a full-time teaching position at a university."

"No regrets, then?"

She rested her chin in her palm, her brow furrowed as if in deep thought. After a long, deep breath, she said, "At first, maybe some. But never about being with our children. It was crazy, almost like having twins, but I wouldn't wave a wand and change any of that."

"What would you change?"

"I don't know." She leaned back, resting her hands on her lap out of sight.

"What's it like being married to a world-famous weapons researcher?"

"Almost as hectic as being home alone with two babies under the age of two. When we're not attending a fundraising event so he can help his company push for more money, he's off somewhere testing and demonstrating. Rick spends over fifty percent of his time traveling."

"You don't go with him?"

"I did, in the beginning, but when our children entered school, we thought it was more important that they have routines and consistency. I mean, yes, we lived in a few different places, but we stayed in those places for at least a year. We decided that when we came to Omaha, we'd stay until they finished high school. That meant one of us — me, would need to be more available for them."

"Doesn't it ever bother you being on your own so much?"

"Not anymore. The kids can handle themselves and I've made a few close connections here."

Her phone vibrated, and she glanced at the screen, then swiped the notification away.

"Are you needed somewhere else? I don't want to take up too much of your time."

"It's fine." She pushed her chair away from the table so she could stand. "I think I will have a coffee. Would you like a tea?"

"No, thanks, I'm good."

Patricia picked up her phone and queued up to order. She reviewed something on her phone, then her thumbs tapped at the screen in rapid succession before returning her phone to the side pocket of her purse. She returned with coffee, a donut, and tea for me.

"Just in case you change your mind," she said, handing it to me and then setting her things onto the table. The chair legs scratched across the floor as she moved closer to the table. "It's like nails on a chalkboard. Sorry!"

"I don't mean to get too personal, but I don't think I could ever be okay with my husband traveling so much. Don't you worry about temptations?"

It was fleeting, but I caught it. The corners of her mouth scrunched, her lips squished together, and her eyebrows turned down, but then she smiled. Patricia Allen Castle was pissed with a capital 'P.' There wasn't any doubt in my mind that she didn't trust her husband. I'd even bet dollars to donuts she knew about his affair.

"Is this the kind of thing that usually ends up in your articles? I was under the impression that this was a serious piece, not for some tabloid rag."

"No, it's not. I'm just projecting, sorry. A series of failed relationships with cheating men and I'm a bit cynical." I shrugged.

She rested her napkin on the empty plate between us and sipped her coffee. Setting it down she said, "Rick has never given me any reason to doubt him."

"You're lucky."

"Yes, I guess I am, but I feel like I really didn't help you with your article very much."

"This was very helpful. I appreciate your time."

"You'll let us know when we can read it?"

"Of course."

"I do need to be going," she said, scooting the chair back.

I stood, shook her hand, and watched as Patricia Castle exited the café and returned to the entrance of Do Space. She stopped at the information counter, then disappeared up the stairs.

AFTER LEAVING DO SPACE and Patricia Castle, I decided it was time to revisit the Kincade store on Maple. I hadn't returned my application and now was the perfect opportunity because Abdul had the morning shift today.

Traveling north on 72nd Street I passed Crossroads Mall, which wasn't so much a mall anymore, but more like a large, defunct retail location anchored by a Target and probably one of the few remaining Barnes & Noble bookstores. The mall had been in a steady state of decline for years, but somehow remained. I heard there are plans to demolish it, but nothing has happened, yet.

Further along 72nd Street, the sprawling campus of Creighton Prep, a school for boys, was on my left. It made me think of Patricia Castle and her kids. They had to be her reason for staying in a marriage that wasn't otherwise working. Of course, maybe there was more to it. Money could be another reason, but all she'd need is a good divorce lawyer, and in Omaha those are easy to find. It had to be about the kids. Unless she's religious. There still are denominations that frown on divorce. Personally, I'm all for it, and not just because I get hired to find dirt on the opposing parties. The way I see it, if you figure out the person isn't a good fit, then it's best to move on, especially if they're a lying, cheating shit. Not being all that religious myself, I've never understood how or why God would want someone to stay in a bad situation.

When I got to Maple Street, I hung a left and continued to 90th Street, still thinking about Patricia and considering God's plan. At 90th, I pulled into Kincade's lot. Rummaging through my satchel, I found the crumpled application, smoothed it as flat as possible, and then filled it in. Abdul was helping a short line of customers, so I waited for them to leave before going inside.

"Hi, remember me?" I smiled and placed the application onto the counter.

"Yeah, yeah," he said this slowly, trying to place why he should know me.

"I helped you with your car the other day. Jumper cables?"

"I knew you looked familiar. Thanks, again. You saved me from being late for class. And that particular professor doesn't tolerate lateness." He looked down, picked up my application, and read through it. "This looks good. I'll make sure the manager gets it."

"Hey, Abdul, can I ask you a few questions?"

"Shoot."

"Everyone else I've talked to doesn't seem too happy working here. Me, I just need a J.O.B., but still, I don't exactly want to work for an asshole, either."

"Mr. Kincade is a character, let's just leave it at that. I've met his type dozens of times before."

"What type is that?"

"Cheap. User," He ticked the traits off with his fingers. "Racist. Low class. Should I continue?"

"Nah, I get the idea. Why'd you take the job?"

"Like you said, it's a J.O.B. I've got another one on campus, but this helps, too. The hours are pretty stable, if you can believe that."

"That's good. I hate when they mess with my hours."

He shook his head, agreeing with my assessment of the state of part-time work.

"What do you think of the other employees? Anybody I should stay clear of? There's always one."

"Everyone is cool, some are just more reliable than others. People at this location are tight. We call each other to cover when necessary, instead of dealing with Kincade or Latrice. We just tell them after the fact. They don't mind because that's one less headache for them. I don't know much about the other locations except Ida. I started at that store."

"Why'd you switch?"

"I got tired of Tate. He's notorious for being late. Gets Monique in fits, which is kinda funny to see. Have you been to the store over on Ida?"

I nodded. He continued.

"Then maybe you saw her. She's small but knows how to throw down. The first time I saw Tate roll in late was during my training with Monique. He strolled in high, like he'd just stubbed out a blunt. She punched him straight in the face. He was so late; she missed a proctored test she was supposed to take. I knew then that I needed to change locations. There was no way I was going to allow some strung out white dude screw with my grades."

"So, is Latrice the manager for all the stores?"

"Unofficially, yes. Kincade never said as much, but she acts the part, and he lets her."

"What is she, twenty-five or something?"

"Nah, she's in her thirties, I think. Been working for Kincade a few years from what Monique told me."

"So, if I get the job, stay away from Ida if I want to avoid Tate. What about that guy Randy? Doesn't he work there?"

"Those two are related, and Randy's always on time. They come from different gene pools, which helps explain a lot about them, but Randy comes in high just about every shift. And I'm sure you know enough about smokin' weed to know that people get the munchies."

"What does he do?"

"They both grab and go all the fuckin' time."

"They steal product?"

"Some might call it stealing."

"What would you call it?"

"They just hungry. I figure they square things up sooner or later, but it's not like Kincade can't afford to lose a bag of chips or two."

Maybe I was wrong about those two after all. Still, the things that were missing weren't always food related. What if they decided to take it a little further? Anybody with a habit needs two things: lots of money and shit to sell so they can get more money. Tate and Randy were back in play.

"What's Latrice like? She cool?"

"She's been known to get into people's business when she shouldn't."

"What do you mean?"

"There's a girl working at the Ida store who everybody thinks is pregnant because of Latrice. She likes to spread rumors. Truth is Keesha, that's the girl, got another job, but didn't want to say anything until she knew if she was going to stay."

"That makes sense."

"Right? Anyway, Keesha's only nineteen, and from what I remember about her, kids are the last thing she wants."

"Latrice also has a tendency to take her unofficial role too seriously."

"How?"

"She tried to fire me when I requested to change locations. And that was the only time since I've been here that I saw Kincade publicly correct her. He likes having a few college students around, even though we're not the color he prefers. Probably thinks it makes him look good to the customers or something."

"There's a lot more drama here than I thought."

"You want your application back?"

Chapter Nine

NOW THAT TATE AND RANDY were back on my radar, I needed to find more details about what they did when they weren't working, besides getting high. Finding their dealer could prove useful, too, and I knew exactly who could help me with that.

I scrolled through my contacts and found her name. We hadn't spoken in a few months since she helped me with a guy problem I was having as a result of finally identifying my sister's killer. She picked up on the second ring.

"Dez?"

"Katrina, I need some information."

"It seems these days you always need something from me. Why is that?"

"Are you going to help me or what?"

"I don't even know what it is you want. How can I be expected to help you with information when I don't know how it's going to be used?"

"I need to know who's supplying over on the northwest side, near 90th & Ida."

"And why do you need this privileged information about my business?"

"It's for a case, or I wouldn't ask, you know that."

"What do you have to trade?"

She always did this. Okay, almost always. When Greg Mitchel, my guy problem, was stalking me, she had my back without question. Her men shadowed me until Murphy confirmed Mitchel was in the wind. So far, he hasn't returned.

"What do you want?"

"One game winner takes Clive."

"Katrina."

"That's the deal. I miss the little man."

I could hear her sipping a drink — probably an apple martini. She liked those fruity drinks.

"You're not serious."

"Oh, fine. You can keep him. How do I know this information won't end up in the wrong hands?"

"It won't."

As far as I was concerned, catching dealers was outside my purview. That business was strictly OPD territory. If I happened to know the name of one, I wasn't under any obligation to share it with them. I wouldn't get anything accomplished if I rolled on people like that.

"You're racking up quite the bill with me, Dez," She paused, and shouted at someone on her side, "Get that shit off the tables and put away. How long should this take?"

"Katrina? When can you get me a name?"

"Come by Easy Street tonight. I'll have it for you then."

"How about we meet at Eddy's instead?"

"You haven't been to see the new layout."

"What time?"

"Ten thirty. I'll leave your name at the door. Dress to impress Dez, it's ladies' night."

The line disconnected, and I already felt the sting of regret. But this was the easiest and fastest way to get information about dealers in and around Omaha. Clive might have known someone who knew someone, but I didn't want to take him back down a road we'd gotten some distance from these past few months since Detrick went away. So far, Katrina had kept her end of the deal, keeping Clive out of the business. Eddy helped on that front and Katrina would never cross him. As tough as she was, Eddy could and would take her out if she came anywhere near his business, and Clive was working for him, which made Clive family to Eddy.

There wasn't much for me to do at this point except wait, so I went to the gym for a quick workout.

THE NAMELESS TWIN CAB trucks at the entrance of Easy Street posted themselves at the head of a lengthy line of patrons eager to imbibe in the many offerings awaiting them inside. Dressed in my favorite A-line little black dress — I only owned one — accessorized with raindrop diamondesque earrings, and my gold shamrock necklace, I strutted to the front. It was cool outside, but I'd decided not to wear a jacket, and had left it in my Jeep. This dress had hidden pockets for money, a key, credit card, a multi-tool weapon, or whatever other small item a woman might feel inclined to carry.

"Name?" His voice reminded me of Mike Tyson.

"Dezeray Jackson."

His hotdog-sized index finger scanned the list and located my name midway down.

"Welcome to Easy Street, Ms. Jackson. Enjoy your evening." He stepped aside, allowing me to pass.

Katrina was correct about one thing, it'd been so long since I'd been to a club, I'd forgotten how the intensity of the music created an artificial sense of desire for anything and anyone. The steady beats rippled through the expansive room, accented by a combination of flashing and blinking lights. The DJ had been relocated since my last visit. Now the booth was in the center of the room, elevated on a platform. As the music intensified, it rose higher until it almost reached the ceiling, then a burst of powder released into the air. Pleasure-filled screams emanated from the dance floor as people raised their hands high, tilted their heads back, and opened their mouths hoping to catch whatever that powder was onto their tongues.

I moved away in search of the bar to ask about Katrina. I assumed she still sat upstairs in a roped off VIP section, but wanted to be sure before taking the climb in my knock-off, zebra-striped Jimmy Choo's from DSW. In a pinch, the heels were a good weapon, and I had to admit they made my short legs look longer.

Pushing my way to the front of the bar, a dark-skinned bartender with an average build and red-rimmed glasses asked for my order. He filled a glass with a French grenache and set it within my reach.

"It's on the house, Ms. Jackson."

I'd never met him before, so I was perplexed as to how he knew my name, but then I noticed the small earpiece.

"Thank you."

"Katrina is upstairs, to the left."

Carefully wading my way through the throng of customers, I found a spiral staircase leading to the second level. At the top, art déco style furnishings allowed for more intimate conversation. A fleur-de-lis iron railing along the perimeter of the upper floor, with tables for two, afforded a perfect view of the spectacle below.

I spotted Katrina lounging on a couch, with her feet tucked to one side, and a Martini in her hand, surrounded by beautiful people. This was nothing new. She wore a pale pink, fitted dress that revealed flawless long, lean legs. She'd dyed her blonde hair red since I last saw her, no doubt deceiving people into thinking she was Irish.

Someone must have said something mildly amusing because Katrina's head tilted back slightly. A smile crept across her face, and I recognized it from years of hanging out together. Whatever had been said wasn't all that funny, and she thought the person was an idiot. She signaled to one of her people who promptly removed the offending party - a man and a woman who did not try to resist or cause a scene.

Katrina saw me, gave an approving head nod to her other guard, and I was allowed to enter the VIP section. The only way anyone knew it was the VIP section is because Katrina sat there. If she had been in the toilet, that would have been the VIP section. I sat in the now empty chair to her left.

"Dez, it's good to see you after so long."

"It's only been a few months. Don't be so dramatic."

"Still, I miss the old days." She set her glass onto a table in front of her and sat back, turning her body toward me.

"No, you don't, and neither do I. Anyone who wants to relive their insecure high school days must be mental."

"You have to admit things were less — complicated."

"True. Also, a lot less interesting. Do you have a name for me?"

"All business, as usual. Your choice of attire is very — how do I put this? Understated, but elegant."

"Katrina, I don't plan on being here all night."

"Why? Are you allergic to a good time? Look around, Dez. This is what healthy, young, sexy people do. You need to live a little."

"I'm good, thanks. I'd rather not get sprinkled with your fairy dust."

She glanced toward the DJ's booth as the crowd beneath roared and more powder dispersed.

"That?" She gestured to the dance floor. "That's nothing, just a little CBD to accentuate the mood. Harmless, really."

"Wow, okay, then." I picked up my wineglass, took a sip, and returned it to the table. "So, who's the dealer I should look for on the northwest side?"

"I did some checking, and it appears that I've had some turnover in that area recently. The new guy is out of Lincoln, one of Pearley's crew. He neglected to discuss the replacement with me. Since Detrick has been unavailable, things have gotten sloppy, but I'm in the process of taking care of that."

"Pearley Santos?"

"That's the one. You remember Pearley, don't ya Dez?"

Fact was, I couldn't forget Pearley Santos even if I'd been struck with a case of amnesia. In my young and stupid years, I had a thing for him. Last time I saw Pearley, the years had done nothing but make him sexier, hotter, and more delectable. If he wasn't a drug dealer, things might have turned out differently.

"He's still alive?"

"Oh, yeah. Still managing the Lincoln market, too. Didn't you see him a while back?"

Katrina knew I ran into him when I helped her with a deal that went all kinds of sideways. By the end, two people were dead — some dumbass professional dude with a family who thought he could screw her over, and a low-level street dealer named Noble.

She leaned forward and reached into her clutch bag on the table, pulled out a small piece of paper, and handed it to me. Opening it, I read the name and an address. I folded it back up and slid it into one of my hidden side pockets.

"Thanks."

"What are friends for?"

I stood to leave.

"At least finish your wine. I know how much you appreciate a good grenache."

"Maybe another time. Thanks, Katrina."

"You know I love you, Dez, even when you're an unappreciative bitch."

THERE WAS NO WAY I would meet up with a dealer wearing a little dress and heels. I stopped by my place to change into something more appropriate, grabbed my gun, and knives. I didn't figure I'd need them, but it's always better to be prepared just in case. Godfrey was happy to see me, mostly because he hadn't eaten since breakfast. I set food and water outside for him, locked up, and returned to my Jeep, the engine still warm.

I secured my gun in a compartment beneath the passenger seat and placed my throwing knives into the one between the two front seats. Checking my cooler, I saw that I was low on water, and decided I should stop en route to get a few bottles. There's nothing worse than being on a stakeout with nothing to eat or drink. Scratch that. The one thing that is probably worse is having to pee so bad your teeth float. I decided to skip the water. I probably would not be out that long looking for Pearley's guy.

The address Katrina gave me had this guy not far from Northwest High School in a neighborhood at 79th and Curtis Streets. It comprised single family, split-entry homes built in the nineties. Real estate in the area went for under two hundred thousand, and it was a perfect spot to sell. Pearley's guy probably had family living in the neighborhood.

Most of the houses were dark with just outside lights on to deter would-be thieves. I parked, turned off the engine, and waited several houses from the dealer's address. It was a school night and parents had to get up for work, but that didn't mean everyone was sleeping.

The first two hours crept along. My body was stiff, and had I been taller, stretching would be impossible. I pulled my legs from beneath the steering wheel one at a time, extended them across the dashboard, and then set them back down. I twisted my trunk left, then right, did a few slow head and shoulder rolls, and sat back against the seat. It was three o'clock in the morning and still quiet.

At four-thirty a light inside a house on the left turned on. Forty minutes later, a man dressed in overalls and carrying an insulated work coat, safety vest, and thermos, got into a Chevy Silverado 1500. I slid lower in my seat as he backed out, with the nose of the truck turned my direction. He sped past me.

My stomach rumbled at around five o'clock, so I grabbed a Colby jack cheese stick and some apple slices from the cooler. All I wanted was to eat and go to bed. Then, another light turned on, this time at the address I was watching. I could see the outline of a woman behind the sheer curtains of what was probably the living room.

The low rumble of a motorcycle eased down the street, then stopped and parked outside the house. The passenger stepped off, removed his helmet, and walked to the front door. I retrieved my binoculars from the glove compartment. He looked like he was maybe sixteen or seventeen years old, with a bleach-blonde buzz cut, and he wore an oversize hoodie. A woman, dressed in a long purple robe, her brown hair pulled back in a low ponytail, opened the door, but didn't invite the young guy inside. He handed her a wad of cash in exchange for a brown lunch sack that he tucked into the back waistband of his jeans. Stepping back, she closed the door, not bothering to wait for her customer to leave. He returned to the bike, hopped back on, and replaced his helmet. The driver sped off and around the corner away from me.

So, it looked like Pearley was using women in his crew nowadays. He was a fairly traditional guy, preferring to keep women where he felt they belonged — cooking, having babies, and hiding their men from the police when necessary. He'd changed a lot since our high school days, and none of that change was for the better.

This dealer's name was Taylor Green. I hated having to walk up on her, potentially in front of her kids, but she obviously didn't care much about them, or she wouldn't be dealing. I got my gun out of its spot and tucked it into the holster beneath my jacket at the back. She had left the living room light on and then another flipped on, probably in the kitchen. I knocked on the front door.

The shuffle of feet, across what I guessed was a linoleum floor, got louder as she approached the door. She was taking her time, and I knew she was looking through the lightly frosted window trying to figure out who was at her door.

"Who is it?"

I debated what was worse, telling her that her former boss sent me, or that her new one did. She had a track record with Pearley and probably knew he wouldn't send someone without giving her a heads up unless there was trouble — the kind of trouble that would get her killed. Not understanding how she left things with him, I opted for the latter knowing that she hadn't met Katrina, yet. Green wouldn't have a reason to fear me. Katrina wasn't known to beat her people until they screwed up. In this case, her issue was with Pearley, not Green. Of course, Green didn't know any of this.

"Dezeray Jackson. Katrina sent me." Silence. Damn, wrong choice.

"I don't know Katrina."

"She knows you. And I'm guessing that's not a good thing."

"Leave."

"I can't do that. Open the door so we can talk. I've got a few questions about some customers."

"I don't know what you're talking about."

"Don't be an ass. Open the door before you wake up whoever else is in your house. This will only take a second, and then I'll be on my way."

The doorknob twisted, and the deadbolt shifted. She opened the door only enough for me to see part of her face. The curve of a security chain dangled, not really preventing me or anyone else from getting inside.

"What do you want? I sent the money."

"What money?"

"Katrina's. I did the drop yesterday. Pearley knows. He can confirm it."

"I don't care about that." I pulled the pictures of Tate and Randy from my back packet. "Do you know these two guys?"

Her eyes scanned the pictures, then she shook her head.

"Are you sure? Listen, I don't give a shit about what you're doing or with who. I just need to know if these two are regulars. You've been in place at least a month, right? Maybe longer."

She started to close the door. I placed my foot in the way.

"Katrina did send me here, but not for you."

She looked at the pictures, again.

"Yeah, they're regulars. Every week at least once."

"What are they buying?"

"Weed mostly, sometimes something a little stronger."

"How do they pay for it?"

"What do you mean? This is a cash-based business."

"They don't have much in the way of cash. Maybe you worked something out?"

Her eyes darted back and forth, and she tried shoving the door shut, again. It was a hunch, and I'd nailed it. Pearley dropped her. Why he didn't take her out for double-dealing, I don't know, but whatever the reasons, she got lucky.

"Who are you to Pearley, anyway?"

Her eyes settled back on me. I heard the pitter-patter of feet behind her. She looked down. A small hand tugged at her robe.

"Pearley's?"

"No."

"He'd never let someone do what you're doing unless,"

"I know one of his brothers."

"I don't care what you're doing, I'm just working a case." I reached into my jacket pocket and then handed her my card. "But I will tell you this, as soon as Katrina checks you out, you're done. You might want to rethink your plan. I've known her a long time."

"They trade crap from that store they both work at."

Chapter Ten

AFTER GETTING THE LOWDOWN from Green about Tate and Randy, I went home to get caught up on some much-needed sleep. Nothing major would happen in the time it took for me to get some rest and reporting back to Kincade. As I drove from northwest Omaha to my place, one thing still nagged at me. How did they go undetected for so long? Kincade was reviewing the security footage and never saw them stealing. Tate and Randy didn't strike me as the strategic types. They were followers, not leaders. They had to have help. My head was too foggy to keep thinking about it, so I turned on the radio.

When I got home, Murphy's Harley was parked close to the garage door still allowing enough space for me to pull in and park. His note had given me the impression he'd be gone indefinitely, and part of me was glad he was already back. I walked inside expecting to see him on the couch, shoes off, feet on the ottoman, and watching the news, but he wasn't there. Godfrey was still outside, otherwise he'd have met me at the door.

"Murphy?"

No answer. I checked upstairs to see if he was sleeping or in the bathroom. He wasn't there, either. Back downstairs, I went into the kitchen, opened the basement door, and listened for a minute.

"Murphy, you down there?"

Silence. Godfrey scratched at the door, so I let him back inside, and brought his food dishes in. Much to his dismay, I didn't have any treats, and he had to settle for his usual dry dog food, He gobbled it up in a few bites, then went to his mat.

Murphy hadn't left any messages on my cell phone, but maybe he'd left one on the office phone. I opened my office door and saw Murphy tied to my chair, head slumped forward, and Greg Mitchel pointing a gun at me.

Hands up in front of my chest, I stopped in the doorway.

"This is only going to end one way, Mitchel."

"Yeah, with you in a body bag and Murphy at the bottom of the Missouri River."

"Senator Ritchie is going away for a long time. Do you really want to follow him?"

"He paid me to complete a mission. I'm completing the mission."

Great, he was a complete whack job.

"Listen, Greg, can I call you Greg? You can walk away now, and no one needs to even know you were here. You can disappear. Hell, I thought you already had."

Murphy stirred distracting Mitchel. I drew my gun and squeezed off a single shot to his chest. The force threw him back into a set of wood bookcases. He stumbled but recovered. I ducked out of the room and behind the corner. I should have known he was wearing a vest.

"Jackson!"

I reached into my jacket pocket for my phone and dialed 911. Godfrey ran into the living room growling as Mitchel stormed out the office. Just as Godfrey jumped at him, Mitchel's gun went off stopping Godfrey mid-jump. He fell to the wood floor with a thud. I ran into the kitchen and out the back door, taking the steps two at a time. The dispatch officer kept talking and assured me that help was on the way. My phone slipped from my grasp as I rounded the railing. Mitchel yelled from the deck. I was out the gate, running to the front. Fumbling with my car key, I inserted it into the Jeep's lock, and swung the door open as Mitchel fired at me from the front stoop. I ducked, jumped inside, slammed the door, and stayed low while attempting to turn the engine over. Sirens screamed in the distance. Mitchel fired again, hitting the driver's side glass. I could hear him running toward the Jeep. I put it into reverse, pushed the peddle with my hands, and hoped I didn't hit anything when I backed up. The Jeep ran up onto the opposite curb.

The screeching of tires skidding to a stop, followed by orders to put the weapon down, sent a wave of relief through my body. I peeked above the dashboard. Greg Mitchel stood in my driveway with his gun pointed at my Jeep. He had me in his sights. His eyebrows furrowed, and he pulled the trigger. I dove back down and covered my head. The officers returned fire. After a minute of Pop! Pop! Pop! I raised up and peered over the dashboard. They'd shot Mitchel in both legs and were in the process of cuffing his hands. Two more patrol cars had arrived. I stumbled from my Jeep, landing on my hands and knees on the sidewalk.

"Are you injured?" Officer Jacobs crouched beside me. When I didn't respond, he asked again.

"No, I'm all right. Murphy. Get Murphy." He helped me stand. "And Godfrey. He shot Godfrey."

Jacobs motioned to another officer, then yelled for them to go inside to find Murphy.

"Jacobs!" The officer returned to my front porch. "Call the bomb squad!"

We looked at each other, then back at the officer. Mitchel lie chest to the ground, chin up, with a grin covering his face.

"Who is this guy, Jackson?"

"Munitions expert. Ex-military."

"Trouble follows you wherever you go, doesn't it?"

Jacobs called for the bomb squad.

MURPHY, STILL OUT COLD, was strapped to a stretcher, wheeled to an ambulance, and taken to Methodist hospital on Dodge Street. Officer Jacobs rushed Godfrey to my vet, Dr. Roberts. The exhaustion I'd felt when I first arrived home was long gone as I followed his patrol car.

Dr. Roberts and his team met us in the lot, moved Godfrey to a gurney, and rushed him inside and into an operating room. I waited in the lobby, pacing.

"Godfrey's a tough dog. He'll make it," Officer Jacobs said before leaving.

For the next few hours, I flip-flopped between pacing and swearing and sitting and swearing. It was one thing for Mitchel to go after Murphy, but to shoot my dog was a different level of depravity.

At one o 'clock in the afternoon, Dr. Roberts met me in the waiting room, his white clothing covered in Godfrey's fur and blood.

"Dez, we've got him stabilized, but obviously he's going to be here for a while so we can monitor his recovery. The bullet went straight through and out the back."

"I understand."

"Why don't you go home and get some rest. You've had one hell of a day so far."

"No, I need to go check on Murphy."

"DEZ, STOP WORRYING, I'm fine." Murphy sat propped up in his bed.

"What the hell happened? I thought you were out of the country."

"I was on my way to meet a client when Mitchel ambushed me. He drugged me, and then must have watched your place until you left. I'm not clear on how he got me into your house or my bike there. Things are still fuzzy. And so far, he's not talking."

"He's cuffed to a bed with two guards posted outside his room."

"Yeah, but they're not telling me where he is."

"Do you blame them? Can't convict a dead man."

"He's a dead man, regardless."

Chapter Eleven

AFTER LEAVING MURPHY, I didn't feel like going home — I was still flying high on adrenaline, so I decided to track down Tate and Randy. Besides work and Chrystal's apartment, the only place I knew I might find them was their apartment. It was off Northwest Radial Highway, not far from Benson High school. Their apartment turned out to be in a converted house. I parked outside a few houses away to assess who came and went. A beat-up Chevy parked in front of their place, caught my eye. It was three in the afternoon, and I expected that most adults would be at work.

The neighborhood was quiet. I reclined my seat just enough, so I still had a line of sight to the front door. I should have known better, because the next thing I remember is the blare of a car horn jolting me awake. My adrenaline high was history. It was three-forty-five, and I had no idea when I'd fallen asleep. Even worse, the Chevy was gone.

I pulled my seat back to its usual position, got out, and walked to the porch. Checking the handle to the door, it turned, and I walked inside. Five feet ahead of me, a flight of stairs led to a second floor. A door to my right was apartment number one. The mailboxes outside showed their place was apartment "two" which, with a cursory examination of the ground level, was upstairs with number three. I climbed the narrow flight, rounded the railing at the top, and found their apartment.

There wasn't any noise coming from inside their place, but I knocked just in case. I hadn't quite worked out my lie when a guy in number three opened his door and peeked into the hall.

"Oh, sorry, thought you was knocking on my door."

"You know Randy and Tate?"

"Nah, not much. Just moved in. Me, not them. They ain't home though."

"You wouldn't happen to know where I can find them, would you?"

"Who's askin'?"

I pulled a card out of my back pocket, walked to his door, and handed it through the crack. He opened the door wider.

"You a PI? For real? Man, that's dope. I don't think I ever met a real PI before, just you know regular cops-n-such. Why you lookin' for them? Oh wait, you prob'ly can't tell me, huh? I understand."

The whole time he talked, I stood there waiting for him to take a breath so he wouldn't pass out.

"So, any idea?"

"Oh, yeah. Sorry. I saw them hanging out at the park down the way. People be shooting hoops and what not." Several dark dreads fell into his face, and he swiped them back.

It was the 'what not' that interested me most.

"Thanks for your help" I said as I moved toward the stairs.

"No problem. Just doing my civic duty," he called after me.

I heard the click of his door as I descended the staircase. The park he was talking about was about five minutes away by car. I'd passed it on my way but hadn't noticed anyone except ballers. But if this guy said Randy and Tate were there, then I was hauling ass to check. I didn't know where else to look for them and hanging outside their apartment wasn't a good idea for me today.

I parked in the only lot in the park, stepped out, and started walking toward the action. Players occupied every court on the far side, but the playground was empty. It reminded me of my NYC days with players exchanging a few body checks and blows before handing over their money.

Randy and Tate sat at a picnic table midway between the playground and the courts, smoking cigarettes and watching the games. When I approached, neither showed any signs of recognition from our previous encounters.

"What's up sexy lady?" Tate said, a plume of smoke escaping his mouth.

"Mind if I join you?"

"It's a free country," Randy said.

I took a spot on the opposite side of the table. Neither turned around.

"You two work at Kincade's, right?"

When they didn't answer I asked a second time. Randy looked over his shoulder, then back at Tate.

"Sexy lady wants to know if we work at Kincade's."

Tate turned his lanky upper body around, his coal-black eyes looking me up and down, then returned his gaze to the courts.

"She looks familiar. She's got one of those faces, ya know what I mean?"

Randy nodded, sloth-like.

"So, I had a little chat with Taylor Green."

Randy sat up and faced me, his pale blue eyes scrunched, and brows drawn down. He extinguished his cigarette on the tabletop between us. Tate followed suit, staring at me.

"Relax." I said, raising my hands palm out in front of me, and leaning back few inches. It's a useful ready position in the event things go sideways. "I'm not here about that. I don't care what drugs you do."

"Who are you?" Randy asked.

Reaching into my back pocket, I produced one of my cards and set it onto the table. Randy's eyes glanced down, then met mine. He pushed the card back toward me.

"Shit, I know you!" Tate said. "You came in the store. Damn, I knew you looked familiar." He slapped the table in victory and kept shaking his head back and forth.

"Mr. Kincade hired me to investigate why his inventory has been coming up short, and from what I can tell that has something to do with you."

"We just," Tate started to speak, but Randy punched him in the shoulder.

"We don't have anything to do with that."

"I'd like to believe you. I really would, but your friend Chrystal said differently."

Randy leaned forward, a line showed the tightening of his jaw muscles, and his hands settled, palm down on the table. The fingers on his left hand twitched.

"Chrystal doesn't know what she's talking about."

"How does she know about Chrystal?" Tate looked at Randy.

"She doesn't know jack."

Our eyes locked for a few seconds longer than what would be comfortable for most people. Tate was still rubbing his shoulder.

"Ya see, here's the thing. I think she does, and you've been bringing her gifts to keep her quiet. Things for her babies, and maybe a little something just for her — to take the edge off."

"It's not like," Tate started to speak again, but Randy interrupted.

"Shut up, Tate!"

"Here's what I haven't figured out, yet." I grabbed my card and returned it to my pocket. "How have you been able to avoid the cameras all this time? Neither of you are trained magicians, so that makes me think that maybe you've had some help."

"We just," Tate scooted out of Randy's reach. "It's just been a few things. It's not like Kincade can't afford it."

Tate underestimated Randy's reach. The backhanded strike to Tate's face almost knocked him off the bench.

"Fuck!" Tate's hands instinctively covered his nose. Blood dripped from it, landing on the front of his sweatshirt. He looked down. "Dammit, Randy!"

"You should pinch that," I said, demonstrating on my nose.

"You don't have any proof, or you wouldn't be here."

"What I have is a dealer's list of crap you've traded, that could probably be tracked back to Kincade's, but like I said, I think you've had help, and I'm more interested in who that is."

Randy wasn't going to roll over on whoever it was, but with enough time alone with Tate, I'd be able to get an answer. I swung one leg over the bench seat, followed by the other, then stood to leave.

"You've got my name. When you're ready to talk, get in touch. It would be in your best interest to do that before I find the person on my own — which I'm likely to do, soon. For whatever reason, Kincade's got a soft spot for you two and I'm betting he'll be more interested in the person who's been covering your asses."

Tate's nosebleed had stopped, and he'd gotten up from the table. Looking down at Randy, he said, "I'm outa here."

"Man, don't be like that. Come on," Randy stood to follow Tate. "I didn't mean to hit you so hard."

I watched as Tate stalked away with Randy in tow, still apologizing.

MY CATNAP IN THE CAR was enough to revitalize me, but I knew it wasn't likely to last long. While I felt alert, I decided to follow-up on something that had been bothering me about my first encounter with Patricia Castle. Whoever called the night we met seemed to unsettle her. The question was, why? Maybe it was nothing, but my brain latched onto it like flies attracted to one of those bug zappers.

From what I knew about her work schedule, she had a night class that ended in about twenty minutes. If I hurried, I'd be able to get there as it wrapped up. As I drove, I developed my cover story. It was going to be something about needing more information about the kinds of activities they did as a family so I could show the softer side of Rick Castle. Public perception of him was along the lines of arrogant, demanding researcher intolerant of other people's incompetencies.

When I arrived on campus, cars streamed from the lot into a two-lane stretch of road leading to the exit. I found a spot close to the primary entrance, parked, and grabbed my satchel. Just as I was about to get out of the Jeep, I spotted Patricia Castle talking with a short, stout-looking man with a beard. I lowered my window to see if I could pick up anything from their conversation, but they were too far away. Reaching into my bag, I retrieved my camera and began snapping pictures.

They stood two to three feet from each other while the man showed Patricia a series of photos. She pointed at one or two of them, asked a question or made a comment, and then tucked the photos into a bag at her feet. She handed him a letter-sized, white envelope. He checked its contents, smiled, and put it into his inside jacket pocket. She turned and began walking toward a vehicle parked several spots from my Jeep. I slid down into my seat and waited for the sound of her engine to turn over before peeking up over the dashboard. The man had left, too, but I hadn't been able to see his car.

The clock on my dashboard read seven-thirty, and I debated between getting something to eat before returning home or eating cereal when I got there. Exhaustion was setting in and making cereal sounded too taxing. I pulled through a Five Guy's drive thru, the aroma of fries wafting through the window as the employee opened it to give me my order, confirmed I'd made the right choice. I set the bag next to me as I drove away, nibbling one fry after another, until my fingers reached the bottom of the bag. By the time I arrived home, I'd finished my cheeseburger and water.

It'd been a while since Godfrey had to stay with the vet overnight, and now, not knowing how long he'd be gone this time, the house felt empty. I walked to the kitchen to toss out my trash, otherwise known to Godfrey as 'evidence I ate without him.' My mind flashed to the moment this morning when Godfrey hit the ground with a whimper. A shudder, starting at my tailbone and ending at my shoulders, surged through me. I wouldn't be sad if Mitchel and a shank became acquainted in the near future.

By nine-thirty, I was in bed with my blanket pulled to my ears and I didn't wake until ten o'clock the next morning. Without Godfrey to force me up to let him out, I slept in for the first time since he came to live with me. I loved the damn dog. Reminding myself of Godfrey's absence and the reason for it soured my mood. I'd slept great, but now I just want to hit something.

AFTER THROWING ON GYM clothes and skipping breakfast, I headed to Simmons to train. I hate working out on a full stomach, especially if I will roll with somebody. The extra weight feels like I'm carrying a sandbag. I know the food realistically doesn't add much — maybe a few pounds, but rolling with guys two and three times my size is more about technique, finesse, and speed, than strength. Extra weight slows me down.

Walking through the doors, the lingering odor of sweat accosted me. Guys lined the walls, watching as Master Simmons explained the intricacies of a Granby roll to escape the turtle position. The class was a mix of beginners up to brown belt, which was typical for this dojang. The demonstration was for the newbies, who Master Simmons would soon pair with more experienced practitioners. By my calculations, the class started thirty minutes earlier. Surveying the room, these guys looked like rag dolls tossed to the bedroom floor after a fitful night's sleep.

Master Simmons gave me a fist bump as I walked past the mats to the locker rooms at the back. I changed into shorts, a rash guard, and wrestling shoes. Master Simmons advocated practicing for the environments a person would most likely encounter. This meant wearing shoes, but since he also didn't want his mats torn up — wrestling shoes. The added benefit was less foot fungus.

Returning to the front, I found a spot away from the group so that I could stretch. After about fifteen minutes, I joined them, pairing with a blue belt I'd met a few weeks back. He knew the Granby roll, but we practiced it anyway, and then moved on to some light stand-up sparring. Before long, the sparring moved to the ground, and ended when he got inside my guard with my arms wrapped around his head and my grip locked onto my arm beneath his neck. I shifted my weight up, tightening my grip. It was one of my favorite chokes. He tapped, and I let go.

"You're evil, Jackson." Sitting back on his knees, he swiped sweat away from his face with his arm.

"Not evil, just determined." I checked the clock above the door. "'Bout that time for me to go. Thanks for rolling with me." I left the mat to go shower, passing Master Simmons office on my way back to the lockers.

"Dez,"

"Sir?" I stopped in the doorway.

"I'm looking for someone to teach a women's self-defense class next month. Two nights or all day on a Saturday. Your choice. You up for it?"

"I'll check my schedule. Can I get back to you later today?"

"Works for me. Nice job out there. You got 'em with that choke, again."

I smiled and nodded.

"Sooner or later, he's going to learn not to let you do that."

"Maybe." I chuckled and made my way to the women's locker room.

Pulling my phone from the top shelf inside my locker, I saw a text message from Susie Walker and I called her back.

"Dez, would you mind coming over to Libby's place this afternoon? I kinda figured that maybe you should take a look at things before I packed them up."

I hadn't bothered before now because I knew whatever was there of importance would have been removed by the police.

"Sure, what time?"

"I'm heading over around one-thirty, so whenever you can after that. I'll probably be there for a while."

"I'm wrapping something else up now. I'll meet you there after I get lunch."

"Great. Thanks, Dez."

Before hitting the showers, I scrolled through my pictures of Patricia and the man she'd met from the previous night. The fastest way for me to find out information about him was to ask Dalton, Haithem's assistant, but I couldn't do that without going to Haithem first. This wasn't exactly a problem, but things between us had been a little awkward since he returned. Our relationship has always teetered on the border between friends or lovers. He flirts and I pretend it's all in good fun. We've been like this for years without ever taking it to the next level. When Murphy came into the picture things got complicated. Then, when Murphy kidnapped him instead of fulfilling a contract to kill him, things between us got really strange.

Instead of calling, I emailed with the pictures attached. By the time I toweled off and got dressed, Haithem had responded.

I'll have Dalton check into this. Look for something from me, soon.

H.N.

LIBBY WALKER'S APARTMENT was located to the south of the Midtown shopping area in a fourplex. It surprised me a nineteen-year-old college student could afford the place. Susie answered after my first knock.

"Dez," Standing to the side of the door, she opened it wider, allowing me to enter. All the furniture in the living room looked new from the forty-eight-inch flat screen TV to the sofa, love seat, and coordinated end tables. The scene came straight from the pages of House Beautiful.

"Where did you say your sister worked?"

Susie gestured toward the living room and kitchen. "All my furniture is used. She didn't have money for any of this."

"What's the rent on this place?" I asked, gazing up at the cathedral ceiling, then out the enormous picture window spanning the length of one wall in the living room. The wall-mounted TV above an electric fireplace opposite the kitchen caught my attention next.

"She never told me."

Stainless steel appliances, and a mahogany stained wood high-top table with matching chairs adorned the kitchen to my left. The stunning blue painted cabinets with black glazing, accented with silver hardware, gave simple elegance to the space. I caught myself thinking I should redo my kitchen to look like this one, but then I remembered that I'm not a DIY kind of person. I also have no inclination to hire anyone to do the work.

Partially filled, neatly labeled boxes scattered throughout the living space told me that Susie had already been here a few hours.

"I'm just going to have a look around, okay?"

She nodded, then returned to one of the boxes labeled "dishes" and continued wrapping plates between sheets of newspaper.

Past the living room, down a hall to my right, I discovered the bathroom. Peeking inside, I saw that it had a whirlpool tub and one of those massaging shower heads I'd, quite frankly, kill for. Fleetingly, I thought I could get Murphy to install one for me.

Further along the hall at the end, I found the door to Libby's bedroom. Inside there was a fully appointed queen size bed covered with those stupid tiny pillows. Put them on, take them off, and repeat. It was an exercise routine I could live without. A hoop draped with mosquito netting dangled from the ceiling, and the sheer fabric flowed over the sides of the bed. I searched through a wardrobe nestled in a corner before moving to the walk-in closet, one side of which contained shelving explicitly for shoes. No compartment remained empty.

For a college kid, Libby had more semi-formal dresses than I would have expected. There was the always useful little black dress, and next to it was a red, then a deep purple, and an emerald green version. Suits filled her closet alongside dress pants and blouses, skirts, and blazers, but not much casual clothing like jeans, T-shirts, or sweatshirts.

Stepping out of the closet, I returned my attention to a nightstand. A dust ring remained where what I guessed was an alarm clock rested. I opened the single drawer, sorted through a few papers, and pulled out a notebook for closer examination. Finding nothing of consequence, I went back to the living room.

"Hey, Dez?"

I turned from a bookshelf I'd been picking through. Susie held a piece of metal, smaller and thinner than a credit card for me to inspect.

"What do you think this is?" She brought it to me.

"Hmm, I don't know. Where'd you find it?"

"There, beneath the couch." She pointed, directing my attention to the side of the couch closest to the kitchen.

The thin metal had a series of numbers and shapes embossed along its longest edge.

"I'm not sure what this is. Maybe nothing. I'll take it with me and see if I can find out anything. Does Libby have any baggies in the kitchen?"

Susie left in search of baggies while I continued my inspection. Looking around the living room once more, I noticed that the north-facing kitchen wall had several pictures and other items hanging from it, but something seemed to be missing.

Returning from the kitchen, Susie followed my stare, pointed to the wall, and said, "There used to be a clock there, but I don't know what happened to it."

"Where was Libby when you found her?"

"Just over there, next to the coffee table." She said, turning her head in that direction.

"How was she positioned?"

"On her back. At first, I thought she was asleep. I know, stupid. Then, when she wasn't moving, I thought she passed out or something, so I tried waking her up."

"What'd you do?"

"I shook her by her shoulders, but she wasn't breathing, so I called 911."

"Do you remember where her arms were positioned?"

"Her right arm was kind of raised to the side, I do remember that. And she wasn't wearing her watch."

"Is that significant?"

"He gave it to her. She never took it off, not even in the shower."

"Maybe the police have it?"

"No. They didn't return it with her clothes or jewelry."

"Can you recall anything else? Anything that seemed unusual or maybe out of place?"

Susie sat on the couch staring at the spot where she'd found Libby.

"Libby was taking anti-anxiety pills. Zoloft. The bottle was on the table, opened, and it looked like several pills were gone."

"That's why this was ruled a suicide."

She nodded her head.

"There were scratch marks on her left arm near her wrist."

"What makes you think they were scratch marks?"

She shrugged and said, "That's what they looked like to me."

"The coroner's report didn't believe that was significant?"

"No. They said Libby might have had an allergic reaction to the Zoloft. They found more in her system than should have been there, I guess."

"Did she have a history of allergic reactions to her medication?"

"No, she wasn't allergic to anything that I know of."

"Was the medicine new?"

"I don't think so. She would have told me if she'd changed it. As far as I know she'd been taking the Zoloft for at least a month, maybe two." Susie sighed, arms resting on her legs, and then her face fell into her hands. After a few deep breaths, she sat up. "Libby wasn't depressed, depressed. You know what I mean? She got a little anxious occasionally, that's all. And she wanted to keep the baby."

"Maybe she changed her mind, Susie. It happens."

A grimace formed across her face as she shook her head in disbelief.

"I know it's difficult to accept, but what the police believe happened might be exactly what happened. You're going to have to accept that possibility."

She stood, pulled the edges of her shirt down, placed her hands on her hips, and took another deep breath.

"These boxes aren't going to pack themselves," she said as her eyes scanned the room. "Thank you for stopping by, Dez. It means a lot to me."

I took that as my cue to leave and walked toward the door.

"I'll let you know if I find out anything more about that piece of metal, but I'm sure it's nothing. Sorry, Susie."

Chapter Twelve

THE REGGAE BEATS OF Bob Marley through my earbuds made the drive to Lincoln Monday afternoon more tolerable. Sometimes I listen to podcasts, but most of the time I let my mind wander as the music plays in the background. There's not much to see between Omaha and Lincoln except an outlet mall and sprawling farmland. Thankfully, the speed limit raised to seventy-five miles per hour several years ago. This means people travel five to ten over that, and if you go with the flow of traffic, you can make it to Lincoln in about thirty minutes or less.

Haithem and I planned to meet at Yai Yia's downtown at two o'clock. His email confirmed that he had an ID for the mystery man in my photos with Patricia Castle, but he didn't say who it was. Instead, he suggested meeting for a late lunch. Knowing I'm a sucker for great pizza, he chose my favorite spot. I also figured I could pick his brain about the metal piece from Libby Walker's apartment.

There is nothing as satisfying as the aroma of fresh-made, cracker-crust pizza. My stomach started doing the happy dance the minute I opened the door to Yai Yia's. Haithem sat on a stool sipping a beer. When he saw me, he stood, beer in hand, and walked over to greet me with a hug. His intoxicating, musky cologne remained in the space between us as we separated.

"Dez, it's lovely to see you. Shall we sit in the back, front, or outside?"

"Back. Less distracting and more private."

"The back it is. Can I get you something to drink?"

"I'll wait until I decide what I plan to order. Thanks, Haithem."

After a few minutes reviewing the pizza menu, I settled on two slices of the Mediterranean and Haithem ordered two of the Milano. That task completed, I ordered a Belgian Blonde pale ale. The bartender handed it to me, and I took a long pull from the bottle.

"How is the pale ale? I haven't had that one."

"Not bad. Should go nicely with my pizza."

We walked the long, narrow length of the space, past the kitchen where the magic happened. Only a few customers from the lunch crowd remained scattered throughout the restaurant. Haithem chose a table in the far-left corner. The chair scraped the wood floor as he pulled it out for me to sit. Before taking the seat across from mine, he removed an envelope from the breast pocket of his grey, slim-fit Hugo Boss suit. He slid the jacket off, folded it, and placed it over the back of the chair next to his. He'd paired the suit with a silk Turnbull & Asser, James Bond-inspired tie. I'd never have known anything about Haithem's wardrobe if I hadn't stayed in his apartment while he was away. He had more clothes than any woman I knew, and most of them were designer labels.

"This is for you."

I opened the envelope, slipped a single sheet of paper from it, and read the information. Patricia Castle's mystery man was an Omaha-based private investigator named Matt Anderson. Dalton included Anderson's contact information. From the sheet, I learned that Anderson had been a PI in Nebraska for the last ten years. Castle hired him three months ago. I didn't understand how Dalton got that last detail, but having worked with him, sometimes it was better not to ask.

"Thanks, Haithem."

"You're very welcome."

"I have one more favor to ask." Rummaging in my satchel, I found the metal piece and handed it to him. "I don't know if there's anything to this, but it was found in the apartment of an apparent suicide victim."

"Apparent? As in, you believe there's more to it."

"I'm not sure. The victim's sister insists that suicide was the furthest thing from her sister's mind. I guess I'm just crossing the t's and dotting the i's."

"How is this related to our Mr. Anderson?"

"Patricia Castle's husband was having an affair with my victim. Now, it looks like she may have known about the affair."

"Ah, of course. This is messy business." Haithem poured the rest of his beer into a glass. "Our line of work can sour a person's view of long-term commitments."

TRAFFIC WAS ALREADY getting thick as I navigated a merge onto I-80, heading back to Omaha from my meeting with Haithem. I squeezed the Jeep between an oncoming semi and the rear of an Outback, then settled into the flow of traffic. Some people prefer ranting and using unfriendly hand gestures during their commute. Not me, though. I pressed the Pocket Casts icon on my dash-mounted phone, then hit play for The Comedy Button.

A few minutes later, I recognized the ring that interrupted my comedy meditation.

"Where are you?"

"In an Uber, on my way to your house to get my bike." Murphy's deep voice filled the car.

"Vacation over, then?"

"Something like that. I need to handle the situation for my client that I was supposed to do before Mitchel showed up. They're not too happy." He paused and gave instructions to the Uber driver. "Where are you?"

"Meeting with Haithem and on my way home now. You going to be there?"

"Probably not. They needed me last week, so it's best if I minimize the damage my impromptu hospital stay may have caused. Any more word on Godfrey?"

"He's stable, but still not ready to come home."

"Mitchel is going to get his when all is said and done."

"Murphy, let the police take care of it."

"Oh, I will, for now. But after he hits the prison yard, all bets are off."

"Look, if anyone should want him dealt with, it's me. It's enough that I know he'll be serving a very long sentence with the general population."

"Dez, a lot can happen before then. He might not even make it to prison. All I'm saying is that if he does, that's where this ends. Mitchel back in the wind isn't good for anyone, especially you."

"He's not going anywhere. They already moved him from the hospital. He couldn't post, so he's locked up. Sometimes friends in high places forget about the ones at ground level."

"I'll keep tabs on it from my end, but you need to keep your eyes and ears open."

"You worry too much."

"You don't worry enough."

The line disconnected, and the show resumed.

Chapter Thirteen

AFTER SPENDING MUCH of my Tuesday morning dealing with a leaky toilet in my basement, and then paying a few hundred bucks for the repair, I returned to the confines of my office to send invoices out. Intermittently, I contemplated a different line of work. Plumbing seemed to be a lucrative business. I dismissed that thought almost as fast as it had entered my head. All it took was seeing a spider crawling up the wall in front of me. Plumbers have to go into crawl spaces, and that's where spiders nested. That was enough to end any fantasy I had about charging high plumber prices.

Meanwhile, the spider continued its climb. I reached beneath my desk, removed my boot, stood, and walked within arm's reach of it. For all I knew, it was a jumping spider. As I raised my boot to smack the spider out of existence, the office phone rang. I leaned over my desk and picked up the handset with my free hand.

"Jackson Investigations."

"Listen, can we meet up?" The voice on the other end barely audible.

"Who is this?"

"Uh, yeah, sorry." The man cleared his throat. "This is Tate. Tate Hill."

"Sure." I grabbed a pen and Post-it note. "Where?"

"Not at work 'cause Randy might show up. And not at the apartment. He's usually hangin' out unless he goes to Chrystal's place."

My pen tapped the note pad while I waited for him to settle on a location. Eventually, he'd get there, but interrupting him would probably act like a reset button.

"How 'bout, I don't know. You pick a spot."

"Okay, can you get to the library at 90th and Fort?"

"Yeah, I can do that. What time?"

"I'll see you there at three-thirty."

I replaced the phone to its charging station. Boot still in hand, I turned to deal with the spider. It was gone.

WALKING INTO THE LIBRARY, I spotted Tate milling about near the circulation desk. A college-age woman smiled and answered whatever questions he posed. Occasionally, she'd sweep her long brown hair from her face and giggle. Tate wasn't a bad-looking guy, just a little too skinny for my tastes. Skinny and stupid.

I approached the desk and tapped his shoulder. He was mid-sentence attempting to tell the girl a joke. It wasn't funny, but she laughed one of those awkward, "I feel bad for you" sort of laughs.

"Tate."

He looked over his shoulder, then returned his attention to the girl.

"So, maybe I could get your number? We could hang out."

She reached for a torn piece of paper — the kind the library cuts up and leaves for patrons to use when they search for a book at the computer stations. The corner of her mouth slid up as she wrote the numbers and then handed the paper to Tate. He pocketed it, then turned to follow me.

"That's not her number."

"What are you talkin' 'bout? Course it's hers. She just gave it to me."

"No, it isn't."

"Wait, how do you know?"

"Private investigator, remember? I get paid to watch people, who believe that they're more clever than anyone else, do incredibly stupid shit most of the time."

"But she did the hair thing."

"She was being nice."

"Man that's f'd up. Women." He sank into a chair along the back wall at the end of a series of shelving. I took the seat next to him. A small, square table rested between the two chairs, and I set my satchel onto it.

"Yep, we're from Venus, apparently." His expression told me the reference was lost on him, so I moved on. "What do you have for me?"

He smoothed out his unwrinkled jeans a few times and adjusted his position.

"Man, if Randy knew I was here,"

"I won't tell him."

"I just don't want to go down for any of it. This was all Randy's idea."

"What was Randy's idea, exactly?"

Tate leaned forward and whispered so quietly, I hardly heard him.

"What? This is a library, not a church, Tate."

"Randy was the one who wanted to pocket inventory and trade it. I mean, sometimes he sells it, but mostly we just trade. That new dealer was the one who offered. The guy before her only took cash, so Randy would take the stuff out of Kincade's, sell it, and then get our weed, or whatever."

"So, what things did you use as a trade?"

"Baby stuff, feminine things, sometimes food."

"Crystal had a black backpack filled with baby items. Was that for her or for Green?"

"Green. Crystal was just hanging onto it for Randy."

"What I don't quite get, Tate is how you two avoided the cameras."

"Latrice."

"Latrice?"

"She made sure we weren't in view. Kincade put her in charge of inventory at all the locations, see?"

I nodded.

"What she'd do is rearrange product and put things in spots so we could get them off camera."

"Why would she do that? What's in it for her?"

He shrugged.

"She's got a friendly relationship with Kincade. I can't see her intentionally wanting to screw that up."

"All I know is that Randy ran into her a few times, and next thing I knew, we was able to grab a few things here and there."

"How long have you had this arrangement?"

"A few months, maybe."

"Why tell me?"

"'Cause maybe you could smooth things over with Kincade. I mean, we didn't take much, and it's not like it was worth a million dollars or nothing."

"Kincade will do whatever he wants to do. I can't help you there."

"But maybe you could tell him it was somebody else."

"You want me to lie and cover for you to the person who hired me?"

The dumbass looked hopeful.

"That's not really my style, Tate."

"What if I could get you more information?"

"Like what?"

"Like what if I got something on Latrice?"

"Go on."

"The last month I been handling a lot of the closings and balancing the money for the Ida store. One night, I was looking over some of the papers and the numbers didn't seem right. I checked back to a few other nights I'd been working. Every time something was off, but only a little."

"How so?"

"It was like chump change, ya know? Like someone made a mistake with their drawer, but it kept happening."

"How far back did you check?"

"A year."

"You checked a year's worth of books and didn't think to tell anyone about it until now?"

"I didn't know who was doing it."

Maybe Tate wasn't as stupid as I thought. I sat back in the chair, taking it all in. If Latrice had been stealing for a year, why'd she suddenly decide to help Tate and Randy? How could she benefit from that?

"What makes you think it's Latrice?"

"She's the one who handles inventory, checks the books, everything. Kincade doesn't do anything except sign our checks. These stores are basically hers, but with a crappy paycheck and a fat boss with grabby hands."

I considered this for a beat. Maybe Latrice was tired of being taken advantage of and opted to take a little something for herself. A little here or there wouldn't get noticed by someone like Kincade. But that didn't explain the inventory. She had to know Kincade would notice that.

"I know you've got to tell Kincade something, but maybe you just tell him about Latrice? Me and Randy don't need to be part of the discussion."

"I can't make any promises, Tate."

When I left the library, Tate had found another young woman to admire. This time, she seemed genuinely into him. The woman at the circulation desk wasn't in her seat as I passed by. Glancing to the computer stations, I saw her assisting a tall, dark-skinned, fit young man with dimples. Tate hadn't stood a chance.

Chapter Fourteen

CUSTOMERS HURRIED IN and out of Kincade's Benson location grabbing donuts, coffee, breakfast pizza, and soda. Some picked up cigarettes, unwrapping them on their way out the door, and then lighting up. It was seven-thirty in the morning and a donut was sounding mighty tasty. I'd been parked outside the store since five-thirty in the morning, waiting for Latrice's shift to start. Now, as I watched, she deftly interacted with her customers. People entered with a frown but left with a smile.

A lull in the action happened around nine o'clock. My stomach rumbled, unsatisfied with the granola bar I'd eaten and washed down with hot tea a few hours earlier. At eleven-thirty another employee started their shift and Latrice disappeared to the back of the store. About an hour later, she exited the store, got into a silver, two-door Nissan, and drove away.

I entered the store hoping to find Kincade and wasn't disappointed. The clerk pointed toward the back office. When I knocked on the closed door, I heard the scrape of a chair across the floor, and Kincade curse.

"Who is it?" His gruff voice boomed through the steel door.

"Dez Jackson."

"Shit, hang on a minute."

When he opened the door, he was wiping something from his pant leg. His desk, which during every other visit had been a cluttered mess, was clear with all the papers stacked neatly to one side. His laptop rested atop a file cabinet to his left. The air smelled salty-sweet.

"What is it, Jackson? I haven't got all day." He returned to the chair behind his desk.

"I'm assuming you have an accountant."

"Course I have an accountant. What do you think I am, a moron?"

Resisting the urge to answer, I waited for him to continue.

"Why do you want to know?"

"Have you had your accountant go over your books recently? Since the inventory issues?"

"I don't pay the accountant to do that kind of thing. I've got Latrice. She does the day-to-day bookkeeping. The accountant does my taxes."

"I think it would be in your best interest to have someone look over your daily accounts going back about a year."

"What are you saying? You don't think Latrice is,"

"I don't know. I'm simply suggesting that you should do your due diligence and have your records checked just to be sure."

"Latrice would never steal from me. She's like a daughter to me."

That wasn't the image I wanted in my head, especially after walking into an office that smelled like sweaty sex. His fingers drummed the table, and a scowl formed on his face.

"I'm sure she feels the same way, but just in case, maybe you should contact your accountant. I think it will be money worth spending."

I left Kincade to contemplate that expense. Before leaving, I bought a chocolate-glazed donut and a Coke. During the quick walk to my Jeep, I'd devoured the donut. Whoever invented the damn things should have served prison time for distribution.

The Jeep roared to life, and tiny drops of rain fell onto the windshield as I pulled out of the parking lot. I still had invoices to get out, so I returned home, but not before checking in with Clive.

He answered on the second ring.

"What's up, Ms. D.?"

"I'm interested in the building."

"Awright! That's what I'm talking about. We can split it up into offices, maybe a little retail,"

"Don't get ahead of yourself. I said I'm interested. First, find out if Detrick will sell it."

"Got ya! I'm on it, Ms. D."

AFTER AN HOUR OF QUICKBOOKS, I thought my head would separate from my body. I closed the laptop, rubbed my eyes, yawned, and stretched. Godfrey's yellow and orange leash dangled from a hook on the wall behind the door.

Dialing Dr. Roberts' clinic, the phone rang five times before going to voicemail. I left a message and callback number. It was past five-thirty, and I knew the office would be closed, but I clicked "two" even though it wasn't an emergency. I missed my dog.

At five-forty-five, my phone rang, and the caller ID told me it was Dr. Roberts.

"Dez? Dr. Roberts here. I've been meaning to call you, but things got backed up here today. Do you have a minute?"

"What's wrong with Godfrey?"

"Nothing to be alarmed about. He's doing really well. Recovering nicely overall."

"But?"

"He's not eating much, yet so we'll need to keep him a little longer. I just want to be sure everything is functioning the way that it should before he heads home. That will make things easier for you both."

"How much longer do you think"

"Let's see where we're at in a few days. You can always stop by the clinic to say hello."

I wasn't sure if he meant to Godfrey or to him, and I was fine with either possibility. Dr. Roberts was single, tall, and hot as a pancake fresh off the griddle. He also had short, dark wavy hair and dimples. I'd never asked about his ethnicity, but I was leaning toward Italian even though his surname wasn't. Everything about him screamed, 'normal and uncomplicated.'

"Okay, I might do that tomorrow. Thanks, Dr. Roberts."

"Not a problem at all, Dez. Have a good evening."

NORMALLY ON A WEDNESDAY night I'd wander over to Brazen Head or Eddy's, but tonight, I wanted to kick back with a glass of wine, eat some popcorn, and watch T.V. The second series of Altered Carbon was on Netflix, and I had binge-watched the first season for the second time to remind myself what the hell happened in the story. It's complicated, kind of like my relationship with Murphy.

Popcorn freshly popped and in a bowl on my lap, with wine at the ready on the table next to the couch, I started the show. Then my phone rang.

"Haithem, it's nine o'clock. Why are you still at work? What would your mother say?"

"Good evening, Dez. I hadn't noticed the time but thank you for letting me know. As for my mother, you've met her. She'd likely ask why I haven't provided her with any grandchildren as yet."

That was true. His mother and father relocated from England to Nebraska to be closer to Haithem and any future grandchildren. They'd given up on his finding a pleasant Arab girl after many failed matchmaking attempts. For the past few years, their sights had set on me. I'd also spent more time with them when Haithem was in hiding, and we'd gotten closer.

"Speaking of your mother and father, how are they?"

"Wondering when you'll be joining them for dinner. I had no idea you visited every week while I was away. It meant a great deal to them. Why didn't you say anything?"

"It was nothing, Haithem. You would have done the same thing for my parents."

"Still, thank you for that. It helped them tremendously. Coping with my supposed death," he paused before continuing, "No parent should go through that. I'm grateful they had you to comfort them."

"Have they forgiven you, yet?"

"They understood that the deception was necessary, but it left a mark." He coughed. "Excuse me. At any rate, that's not why I've called. I have some news for you about the piece of metal you found."

I set the bowl onto the table next to the couch. Haithem continued.

"As you are aware, it is a very thin metal alloy, however, it is not just one, but two. We were able to separate them to reveal a small circuitry."

"For what?"

"That I cannot say for certain at this point."

"Could it have been part of a clock? Something like a wall clock?"

"Hmmm, that's an excellent question. Most of the internal workings of a clock would not have a need for something like this."

"So, if it was inside a clock then it was for something else."

"Exactly, but why are you thinking it was inside a clock? It could have fallen out of something else."

"Libby Walker had a wall clock, but it's not there now. And I didn't see anything in the immediate area that would make sense."

"Depending on the size of the clock, and the housing on its back, this piece could fit inside, or have simply been placed on the back, but there is no tape residue."

"Probably held inside, then. "Yes, in all likelihood."

"Thanks, Haithem. I owe you."

"Dinner, Dez. You still owe me a dinner."

Chapter Fifteen

AFTER SOME BACK AND forth with Rick Castle's assistant, I scheduled an appointment for ten-thirty this morning. I gave her a story about a looming deadline that I couldn't miss, and an unreasonable editor. She must have been able to relate because after ten minutes of saying she couldn't fit me into his schedule, suddenly there was an opening.

I had a few hours before then, and since I had heard nothing from Kincade, yet there wasn't much I could do on that front. This was a rare moment, and I didn't know what to do with myself. Usually, I'm up to my eyeballs in paperwork and invoicing, but since hiring Clive, some of that work became his. He was a quick study and kept meticulous notes.

The house still was too quiet without Godfrey. When I stopped by the clinic yesterday, he perked up when he saw me, but didn't have enough energy to raise himself off his bed. I sat on the floor, rubbing his head, and telling him all about the neighbor's new cat that I was sure he would love. Eventually, his eyes closed. When I heard the tell-tale snoring, I knew it was okay for me to leave.

Now, I surveyed my empty house, making a mental note of all the chores that had gone undone the past week. Stacks of magazines and newspapers covered the dining table; I'd used them while researching a case last month. A laundry basket filled with unfolded, clean clothes rested on a chair. Another basket with dirty clothes hadn't made its way to the basement. As I picked up the dirty laundry and walked toward the kitchen, I noticed a thin layer of dust had settled on bookshelves that lined a wall in the dining room.

"Nope, not today," I said, and continued to the basement.

***

"MS. JACKSON, IT'S A pleasure to see you again." Rick Castle met me in the main lobby. We did the obligatory handshake before he guided me to a compact conference room at the top of a flight of stairs. From this vantage point, I could see everyone in the central lobby except anyone who'd gone to the bank of elevators.

"We're just in here," he opened the door and allowed me to enter before him, then closed it saying, "Sit anywhere you like."

I pulled out the chair at the head of the table and tucked my satchel onto a seat to my left, before sitting. Rick Castle took the seat to my right.

"My assistant indicated that you have a deadline looming and needed some additional information. I don't have much time — my own deadlines to meet. I'm sure you understand."

"This won't take long at all." I smiled and nodded reassuringly.

Reaching into my satchel, I pulled out a notebook and pen, set it in front of me, and then grabbed my phone. Scrolling to my gallery, I clicked on a picture of Libby Walker. I set my phone onto the table in the space between us.

"I understand from Susie Walker that you know her sister, Libby Walker."

Castles eyebrows furrowed, causing a crease to form between his eyes. His back straightened as his gaze moved over the image.

"Susie Walker has asked me to look into her sister's death."

"W-what is this all about? Surely this isn't part of your article."

For a smart guy, he was slow. I removed a card from the front pocket of my bag, slid it across the table, and waited for this new information to register. Castle examined it, picking it up, turning it over a few times, and then slid it back across the table to me. The crease between his eyes deepened and the edges of a scowl formed.

"What the hell is this about?" He said this with a calm that defied the edginess his body revealed.

"As I said,"

"I heard what you said."

"I'm investigating the apparent suicide of Libby Walker. Her sister mentioned that you and Libby were seeing each other before she died."

He scoffed. "Seeing each other?"

"Yes."

"It was a fling. That's all. And the articles I've read confirmed that she killed herself."

"How long were you seeing each other?"

He pushed his chair from the table so that he could stand.

"I don't need to talk with you about any of this. This meeting is over." He stepped to the door.

"I suspect the police don't know about you."

His hand had just reached the door handle, but he stopped and turned back.

"Why would they? She was obviously distraught."

"Still, they might find it interesting to know that she was having an affair with a married man before she died. That could shed fresh light on the entire situation."

"It was a mistake, that's all. I ended it."

"Before or after she told you she was pregnant?"

I could see the whites of his eyes and a flash of worry swept across his face, but then it disappeared. His hands smoothed his lab coat, and he returned to his chair.

"She planned to have an abortion, and I told her I would pay for it."

"Susie said that Libby was happy about the baby."

"She's wrong. Libby was relieved when I told her I'd take care of the problem. She was nineteen years old, for Christ's sake. She didn't want to be tied down with a baby in her first year at university. We were careless, that's all."

"Why did you end the relationship?"

"The fling had run its course. By the time she told me about the pregnancy, we hadn't seen each other in weeks."

"How was she when she told you?"

"How do you think she was? I told you, Libby didn't want the baby. She was relieved."

"How long did you say your relationship lasted?"

"About six months."

"How did you learn about her suicide?"

"Like most people, I suppose. It was in the paper. As far as I understand, there's absolutely nothing suspicious about her death. She was taking antidepressants."

"Susie mentioned that. Was Libby taking her medication regularly? I mean, you were around her quite a lot during those six months. You must have noticed."

His right hand floated to his chin with his fingers lightly covering his mouth, and his index finger tapped his lips. "I'm sorry, I really can't help you. Yes, she was taking something, but what and how long — I don't really know. She was clearly more troubled than I realized." He reached for my card. "If I think of anything that might be useful, I'll call you."

"What about your wife?"

"Excuse me?"

"Have you told her about the affair?"

He shook his head. "She doesn't know. Honestly, this is the first time something like this has ever happened. That's really the reason I ended things with Libby."

"What is?"

His shoulders, that up to now had been tense, sank.

"The guilt. I know I'll have to tell her, eventually."

That light must have been flashing on my forehead, letting him know the psychiatrist was in, so I rode with it.

"Your wife seems to be a very patient woman."

"She is, and she's always been supportive."

My inside voice spouted off. Then why'd you cheat, asshole? Seriously, what was wrong with this man? He has a devoted wife following his dreams with him, all the while forsaking her own. What does she get in return? A husband who can't keep his penis in his pants. And that, ladies and gentlemen, is precisely why I'd make a crappy therapist.

I took a deep breath and began putting my things back into my bag. "Thank you for shedding some light on this." Rolling the chair back, I stood to leave.

"I am sorry about Libby. You'll tell her sister for me, won't you? I couldn't attend the memorial service — for obvious reasons, but I would have like to, and I did send flowers."

"I'll be sure to share your condolences."

AFTER MY MEETING WITH Rick Castle, I thought I'd try my luck with Matt Anderson. I wanted to confirm my suspicions that Patricia Castle knew about the affair. I enlisted Clive's research skills to track him down. Apparently, Anderson favored dive bars for lunch. On this particular day, I'd find him at a place called Lucky 7 in South O.

Traveling along south Thirteenth Street, I passed Sokol Auditorium, the best spot for up-and-coming touring bands. It'd been a few months since my last visit. I can't remember the name of the group, but the place was wall-to-wall bodies. Some guy who knew a guy who knew another guy, got free tickets for Murphy. It's standing room only with an upper level for people who will pay a little more. Our tickets got us ground floor access, but I wasn't complaining. The only negative is the lengthy lines for the women's bathroom. Of course, that'd be true in an upscale location, too.

The Lucky 7 bar was a few blocks south of Sokol on the west side of the street, tucked between a gas station and a laundry mat. I'd never had a reason to go inside the place until now. I parked a half block up the road, locked the Jeep, and heel-toe expressed it back to the bar. A few patrons hung around outside smoking cigarettes and clouds of smoke engulfed the entrance.

In the dimly lit room, several wood tables with mis-matched chairs occupied every available inch of space. Instinctively, I scanned for additional exits. There was a kitchen, so I knew there'd be one in that direction, but other than that, the way I came in was the only other way out.

Several men sat at the bar knocking back shots with beer chasers. I figured they were celebrating something. There were two women working the already crowded tables. One wore jeans that betrayed her bulging body and a Lucky 7 t-shirt two sizes too small. I guessed she was around forty years old. The other woman was younger, maybe closer to thirty-two. She wore bedazzled jeans, pointy cowboy boots, and the same Lucky 7 t-shirt. The lunch rush was in full swing.

I spotted Anderson sitting at a booth in the corner furthest from the door. One of the women had just delivered his burger, fries, and what looked like a two-finger whiskey with a beer. Matt Anderson was a short, round man with blotchy red skin behind a greying beard.

"Mind if I join you?"

Head nod. I slid onto the bench seat opposite him.

"What's good here?"

"Do I know you?" His voice was raspy and deep.

"Dezeray Jackson." I slid my card across the table, placing it in front of his plate. He glanced at it, then returned his attention to his food.

"Is that supposed to mean something to me?" He popped a few fries into his mouth, then drank some of his beer. After biting off a piece of his burger, a mixture of ketchup and mayo dripped into his beard. He grabbed a napkin to clean it up, then tossed it onto the table.

"I think you're working with a client named Patricia Castle."

"What about it?"

"I'm working a case that might involve her husband, and I'm curious why she hired you."

Anderson took another bite of his burger. Mouth still full, he said, "I'm not gonna tell you that. I don't know you from boo."

"I can appreciate your desire to be discreet."

A server wandered over to check on us.

"Can I get you something to eat?" She smacked her gum as she balanced an order book and pen in one hand, and tray with dirty dishes in the other.

"Nah, I'm good, thanks."

"We got chicken fried steak on special today. It's real good."

"Ya know what, I'll take it to go."

"It comes with cheesy potatoes and green beans. You want that?"

"Sure, that sounds great."

"It'll be about fifteen minutes," she said, then left.

"What's your case?" Anderson asked.

"Suicide."

"Oh, that's ugly. What's the husband got to do with it?"

"Now see, if you were in a sharing mood, then I'd be happy to tell you, but,"

"She thought he was porkin' some girl."

"Was he?"

"Not one," he said, shoving a fry into his mouth.

"How many?"

"Two that I know of so far. Anna Summers and CeCe Stiles."

"Who are they?"

"Both undergrads. Summers was at UNO. Stiles is at Creighton. What's the connection to your suicide?"

"Not sure, yet. He was having an affair with her, and the sister doesn't believe it was a suicide. She's convinced Castle had something to do with the death. You said Summers was at UNO." He nodded. "Where is she now?"

"Not sure and it really wasn't germane to what my primary objective was. All my client paid me to do was see if her husband was having an affair. I did, and he was. She didn't pay me to go on a 'where are they now' discovery tour."

Anderson drained his whiskey and signaled for another. The server, already on her way to deliver my order, double-backed to grab his drink from the bar.

"That Rick Castle is a piece of work. I'm betting my two, and your girl are the tip of the iceberg," he said, wiping his hands and face before reaching for his whiskey. "I'll tell you what, these rich people got too much time on their hands."

Chapter Sixteen

"JACKSON, YOU WERE RIGHT!"

It took me a few beats to recognize Kincade's voice. I moved my cell phone in front of my still sleep-filled eyes to check the time. It was five-thirty in the morning. What the hell was he doing calling me at this hour? I tapped the speaker icon and set the phone back onto the nightstand.

"Oh, yeah? About what?"

"Latrice. That conniving Black bitch has been skimming money from me for at least a year."

"Sorry to hear that."

"That doesn't explain the missing inventory. I've been over those recordings. You've seen 'em, and I had my attorney check them out. There's nothing on them to prove Latrice had anything to do with that. I need you to get me proof. I'm going to nail her ass."

I rubbed my eyes and pushed myself upright, swinging my feet over the side of the bed to the floor. Kincade was a bigot and an asshole. There was no disputing that, but Latrice was stealing. It's times like these when I wish I didn't find the truth. I wish I could tell him something that would get the heat off her. She had kids to support and a husband who was killed by a drunk driver. I'd like to believe that everything she did was just her survival instincts kicking into high gear.

"Are you still there? My accountant says she stole at least ten grand. Add the inventory to that, and,"

"Yeah, I'm still here. Kincade, have you ever considered that maybe if you paid people what they're worth, you wouldn't get screwed over?"

The words fell out of my mouth before I could catch them, but in all honesty, I didn't much care.

"I pay her better than most and what does she do with my generosity? She deserves what she gets. Nig,"

I hung up before he finished the next syllable. I hadn't planned to get up this early on a Saturday, but here I was. Usually I'm a "get in, get out" shower person, but this morning I needed a massage. The water tumbled onto my shoulders and streamed down my backside. Leaning my hands against the shower wall, I breathed in the peppermint-scented soap. I switched to it because it was supposed to be invigorating. All I wanted to do was crawl back into bed.

Stepping from the shower, hair wrapped with my Luxe microfiber towel, I dried the rest of my body, and applied a thick layer of cocoa butter. Ash is real and the cool temperatures had already taken a toll on my legs. I pulled on a pair of faded jeans, a black mock turtleneck, and my boots before pulling my hair back into a low ponytail. Seeing my reflection, I didn't look as exhausted as I felt, so I moisturized, added a light foundation and Burt's Bees colored lip balm, before heading downstairs to the kitchen.

My brain was still working through ways to get out of giving Kincade what he wanted. I popped an Everything bagel into the toaster and made Breakfast Serenade tea. The only good bagel is one smothered in cream cheese. A little fat never hurt anybody. Besides, if I skipped this part, the bagel would taste like crap because I'd burned it. It wasn't a piece of charcoal, just more singed than I usually liked.

As I entered my office, balancing the plate, tea, and some stray files I'd left on the kitchen table, the phone rang. Clive's name appeared on the caller ID. Setting everything down, I grabbed the phone on its third ring.

"What'd you find?"

"Good morning, Ms. D."

"Good morning, Clive. What you got for me?"

"Nothing on Anna Summers, yet. But Cece Stiles is still at Creighton. I texted you her class schedule. She also works at a restaurant in the Old Market, so, you know, we could check that out."

Lately, Clive had been eager to get into the field. When he started working for me, I kept him confined to research, and only the occasional surveillance, but never without me. I knew he'd catch on quick, but I wanted to keep him off the street during Detrick's trial. With Derrick off the streets, it made his family an easier target even with Katrina's protection.

"I'll swing by to pick you up in twenty. Be ready to go."

"After we can check out the building, maybe do some pre-planning."

"I haven't decided about the building. Besides, what'd Detrick have to say about selling it?"

"Yeah, about that,"

"What, Clive? Spill it."

"It turns out the building was never in his name."

"Who owns it, then?"

"Me."

"Why would you want to sell it?"

"Detrick had things set up to pay all the taxes and shit, but I don't have money for that unless the building has tenants, but since that can't happen, you know, immediately, I thought me and you could be partners."

"Partners?"

"Yeah, you know, I sell you an interest in the property, you take care of the taxes until we get it rented."

"I'll be there in twenty."

I hung up.

Partners? The idea didn't thrill me. If I was going to buy the building, I'd just take it outright, but it sounded like Clive wanted to keep it now that he knew it was his. Of course, I had leverage since he couldn't afford to pay the taxes. I'd have to think on it a little longer. If anyone deserved a do-over in life, it was Clive. That's why I took him in, so I could train him into who he wanted to become. Being a successful low-level drug and art forgery dealer gave him an attractive skill set when it was combined with book smarts. He wasn't impulsive and understood the importance of patience and strategic thinking. Maybe it was time for him to visit one of Tracer's training facilities after all. I'd held off on recommending him just to make sure he had the drive for the work. Over the course of the past several months, he'd demonstrated that. Before leaving, I left a message for Haithem.

IT TOOK LONGER TO FIND a parking spot than it did to drive to the Old Market from Clive's place near Cuming Street. By the time we did, sprinkles tapped my windshield. Rummaging through a pile of bags behind my seat, I found an umbrella and handed it to Clive.

"Don't you want one?"

"I won't melt."

We walked a block north to the main street through the Market and headed east. CeCe worked at an Italian bistro that'd opened a few months back. Cynthia and Mick raved about their fresh mozzarella and handmade ravioli, but hadn't tried their breakfast offerings. We waited outside, pretending to read the menu while getting eyes on whoever was already inside.

"Ya know, I was thinking 'bout applying to university." Clive said nonchalantly as he reviewed the breakfast list.

"Really? What's stopping you?"

He shrugged with his hands tucked inside his front pockets, and the umbrella held in place between his arm and side.

"What are you thinking about studying?"

"Law."

I looked at him sideways. He caught my eye and grinned. Clive had perfectly straight, brilliantly white teeth. They were a striking contrast to his skin tone.

"What kind of law?"

"Criminal."

I turned toward him and shoved his shoulder. "You're shittin' me. Criminal law? Really?"

"Yeah, I mean I already know something about it, so I figure, why not?"

Looking through the front window, he said, "That's her coming from the back."

CeCe Stiles had long, blonde hair. She wore a flower print skirt coordinated with a light green shirt and cropped jean jacket. Stopping at a table near the back, she distributed water to its occupants before moving to another table.

"You hungry?"

"You ain't got to ask me twice." Clive reached for the door, opened it, and waited for me to enter.

A sign posted near the door read, "Sit anywhere you like," so I picked one in the section I thought belonged to Stiles. Before long, she came to our table, water on a tray, and menus tucked beneath one arm.

"Here you go. We make the cinnamon rolls fresh every day and they're filling! But if you're famished, then you can go the more traditional route for breakfast." She pointed to a few egg and pancake combinations.

Clive went the traditional route while I ordered the roll with tea. Stiles smiled approvingly, retrieved the menus, and scurried off to the kitchen to turn in our order.

"How you wanna do this? I say we eat first. She's not going anywhere."

"I figured you'd want to do that."

"We gonna try to talk to her in here?"

"We'll see how it goes after I introduce us. She might be uncomfortable talking about Castle, especially with so many ears open. Just hurry up with your food so we're ready to move if we need to."

"There you go." The cinnamon roll filled the entire plate, and not just the center, but edge to edge. She laughed. "You might need a to go container." She set Clive's food in front of him, then disappeared to the back, again.

"If you can't finish that," Clive smiled from across the table, then took a bite of his bacon.

"Stop eyeballin' my roll and eat your own food. You got plenty!"

Twenty minutes later, I'd barely made a dent in the roll, but Clive's plate was clean. He pushed back, placed his hands on his stomach, and patted it.

"Damn, that was good. You still eating that?"

CeCe returned with our check and a box for my roll. She scooped up my plate, slid the roll into the container, and set it back onto the table. "Just pay whenever you're ready. There's no hurry." She began clearing Clive's dishes, setting them atop my plate.

"Ms. Stiles, my name is Dezeray Jackson. This is my associate, Clive Dixon. We're wondering if you might have a minute to talk with us about Rick Castle." I handed her my card.

She almost dropped the stack of dishes. Clive reached for them, steadying her hand.

"Um, I - I don't know how I can possibly help you."

"Is there somewhere more private where we can talk?" I looked around. It wasn't sprinkling or raining, yet. "Perhaps outside? This will only take a few minutes." I gestured toward the door. She set the plates down.

"Just give me a second to ask someone to cover for me."

A short time later, Clive and I followed her out. Moving away from the entrance, she walked toward the corner at the east end of the block.

Turning to face us, she asked, "What's this about?"

Sidestepping that question, I asked, "How long were you seeing Rick Castle?"

"Not very long. A few months."

"Who broke off the relationship?"

"I did."

Clive had already pulled out his notebook to jot down whatever CeCe planned to share with us.

"Why did you end it?"

"I can't really explain it."

"What is there to explain?"

"Something just seemed, I don't know, off. When I met him, he told me he planned to leave his wife. I didn't really believe him. I mean, I think I wanted to, but I knew the odds weren't in my favor."

"Did his wife know about you?"

"I don't think so."

"So why end it?"

"When we first met, I was involved in several activities and volunteering — that's how we met. He attended a fundraiser for an organization where I volunteered. I thought dating an older man would be exciting and interesting, especially someone like him. One thing led to another,"

"And then you ended it."

Her hair had fallen in front of her face. She swept it away. "At first, I thought I was tired all the time because I was busy. So, I cut back on my hours. I still felt strange — kind of like I was in a fog a lot of the time. And the headaches, those were the worst part."

"What did that have to do with Rick Castle?"

"He wasn't very supportive when I tried explaining how I was feeling. His suggestion was that I keep a little notebook handy and track my moods. I just thought that was a strange way to respond. My friends kept telling me to see a doctor."

"Did you?"

"Yeah, eventually, but she couldn't find anything wrong. She ran some tests and suggested I see a counselor."

"A counselor?"

"I was beginning to feel paranoid, like someone was always watching me. It made no sense. But the more I thought about things, and talked to my counselor, the only thing that was different was my relationship with Rick."

"Was he saying or doing something to feed into your feeling of paranoia?"

"Other than constantly telling me to write things down with the date and time, no. I guess I should have guessed he'd look at my problem from a clinical perspective. I just — well, I didn't like it, so I ended things."

"Why were you so shaken when we first asked you about him?"

"A month ago, Rick showed up at my apartment. He made some excuse for stopping by. I'd just gotten out of the shower, so I let him in and returned to my room to get dressed. When I returned to the living room, he was gone."

"That is strange."

"That's what I thought. He didn't leave a note or anything. And my watch was missing."

"Watch?"

"He'd given it to me as a gift. Who does that? Who gives someone a gift and then takes it back? It seemed petty."

"Yes, it does."

I thanked CeCe for her time, and Clive and I walked back to my Jeep. Inside, Clive flipped through the pages of his small spiral notebook.

"Didn't you say that Libby Walker was missing a watch?"

Chapter Seventeen

THERE'S NOTHING QUITE like sleeping in on a Sunday morning, not that I would know since my ass was sitting outside Latrice's apartment debating whether I should intervene. Kincade was using her, and now that he knew she used him back, he was out for blood. I'm not advocating stealing from your employer — that shit is just stupid, but I also can't sit back and watch some good-for-nothing racist white dude screw with someone's life just because it gives him a hard on. I sipped my tea, ate a raspberry-filled donut with icing, and waited. I didn't know much about Latrice other than her husband was killed, she had kids to support, and she worked for Kincade.

It was almost nine o'clock and I could see movement inside her apartment. At nine-thirty Latrice, followed by three kids who all looked under the age of ten, left her building. The youngest held her mother's hand as they walked to the corner bus stop. A short time later, the bus arrived, and they boarded. Tailing a bus is a serious pain with all its starts and stops. Trying to stay behind and a few cars back isn't easy. Eventually, Latrice and her crew stepped off the bus a block away from a church in North Omaha. People are strange. I could never understand traveling so far just to go to some church.

I parked across the street a half block away with a full view of the entrance. The pastor and a woman I assumed was his wife, stood outside greeting people as they entered. The women, dressed ornately in their two-piece Sunday best with matching hats, flowed inside with the occasional glance to check each other out. The men, not to be outdone by the ladies, showed up in style sporting colorful suits accessorized with bow ties and precisely folded pocket squares. The entire spectacle was reminiscent of Fashion Week in NYC. Knowing that this could turn into a full day sitting on my butt inside the Jeep, I packed plenty of snacks.

By two o'clock my bladder was a balloon about to pop. There weren't any gas stations near the church, so I either had to do the chair wiggle or go into the building. Going inside was as appealing as stepping on Lego pieces in the dark.

In my experience, entering any church led to heavy recruitment efforts by the congregants. They'd try to disguise their ploys, but the result always was the same. I'd nod and smile and insist that I was just visiting because I wasn't really from the area. This usually worked unless it was a mega church with a national presence. Then the member would share everything I didn't want to know about their church in whatever state I said I was from. I started saying I was from Alaska, but then met someone who attended a Baptist church there.

Just as I mentally committed to braving the onslaught of churchgoers, congregants began filing from the building, and saying their goodbyes. Relief swept over me. I spotted Latrice with her kids heading back to the bus stop. Stepping out of the Jeep, I jogged to catch up with her.

"Latrice?"

She turned, and recognition slowly crept across her face.

"Aren't you the lady Kincade hired?"

"Yeah. Listen, can we talk? How about I buy you and the kids some ice cream?"

"What do we need to talk about?"

"I think you probably already know."

She shook her head and said, "I don't have anything to say to you."

"Mama, the bus is comin.'" Her middle child tapped on her mother's arm, while holding onto her younger brother's hand. The oldest had found something on the ground to occupy his attention.

"Look, I understand men like Kincade. He's not going to let this ride. How about we talk and see if I can help you navigate this a bit?"

Latrice hesitated before answering, glancing back toward the church to assess whether eyes were on us.

"Fine," she said.

We walked back to my Jeep and then I realized we needed at least one car seat for the youngest. I figured we could get away with the other two in belts.

"Does anyone in your church have a car seat we could borrow?"

"I don't know." Her gaze returned to the front doors where members lingered on the stoop engaged in idle chitchat. "They get a lot of donations. I'll go check." She left the two oldest in the Jeep and carried the youngest with her. A short time later, Latrice stepped out of the building carrying a car seat.

Handing it to me, she said, "They have more shit than they know what to do with. Said I could keep this one."

Secured and ready for its occupant, I let Latrice get him settled. He fussed a little at the snugness of the straps but gave up when Latrice gave him a butt-smack warning.

I drove downtown to the only ice cream place I could think of. It didn't hurt that it also was the best place in Omaha to get homemade ice cream. I figured the kids probably hadn't been there before and the newness would keep their attention while Latrice and I discussed the recently surfaced problem. Cooler temperatures didn't dissuade anyone from buying ice cream from Ted & Wally's. The full parking lot was evidence of that. After about ten minutes circling the block, I finally found a spot.

"Mama, what's this place?" The oldest asked, scanning the street and then investigating the outside of the building as we approached.

"The best ice cream in town," I said, smiling. "You like ice cream?"

All three children shouted 'yes' as smiles spread across their faces. When we reached Ted & Wally's, the line wound from the counter to the inside of the door, so we had to wait outside for a few minutes.

"What kind they got?" The middle girl asked.

"I don't know. We'll have to wait and see because they make the ice cream from scratch. It's different all the time. I'm hoping they have Kahlua."

"I hope they got chocolate. I only like chocolate," the girl said.

"I don't care what they got. I'll eat it all!" The older one said.

"I want 'nilla! I want 'nilla!" the youngest spoke over the older boy.

"Hush!" Latrice admonished.

At the counter, I bought a single scoop in waffle cones for the older two, a double for Latrice, and a sugar cone for the youngest. To my delight they had Kahlua, and I ordered two scoops. I grabbed a pile of napkins before sitting at a booth with a view of the lot. The oldest slid into the seat before me, and the others sat opposite with Latrice. As the children focused on devouring their treat and talking with each other about how good it was, I broached the subject of Kincade.

"I know what you've been doing and about how long you've been doing it. So does Kincade. If you can get ahead of this, you might not have any time away."

The reality of what I'd said registered on her face. It was as if this was the first time she considered that she might get caught.

"We're talking about at least ten thousand dollars. Do you know how much time that carries?"

She shook her head.

"Kincade isn't going to care why you did it or how long you've worked for him. None of that matters."

"I've been loyal to that son of a bitch for a long time. When their father died, do you know what he did?"

I shrugged.

"Nothing. Not a goddamn thing. When I didn't show up for my regular shift because I had to take care of funeral arrangements. Do you know what he did?" The children, sensing the tension, stopped eating their ice cream. I could feel the stare of the older boy.

I shrugged, again.

"He told me that if I didn't get my black ass to work, then I was fired."

"I think we agree that Kincade is an a—," All eyes on me I continued, "Butthead. Here's the thing, what you did was I-L-L-E-G-A-L."

"Illegal?" The older boy looked from his mother back to me.

Who knew a second grader could spell so well?

"Mind yer business and eat your ice cream," Latrice said. "There ain't nothing I can do, then." Tears formed in her eyes. I hate it when people cry.

"I can help you."

"Why would you help me? You don't even know me."

"Look, I know you've been dealt a crappy hand and I also know that before this job at Kincade's you were going to nursing school. Right?"

She nodded. Ice cream dripped onto her hand, and she grabbed a napkin, then handed the rest of her cone to the older boy. This caused a grumble from the girl which Latrice promptly shushed.

"I'll take care of Kincade, but you need to find another job."

"How?"

"How, what?"

"My car was totaled in the accident, and I haven't had enough money to get another one. That's one of the reason's I took the job at Kincade's. Buses take forever, and with the kids," She slumped into the back of the booth.

I reached into my jacket pocket, pulled out a sheet of paper and handed it to her. She leaned forward, elbows resting on the table, and opened it.

"I did some checking around. College of St. Mary's has a program that might be able to help you. It's called Mothers Living and Learning. You and your kids can live on campus. Call that number."

"I don't understand. Why are you doing this?" Tears streamed down her cheeks. She swiped them away with the back of her hand.

"Latrice, I'm a 'three strikes you're out' kind of person unless that person is a real—" I looked at her kids. "Screw up. You don't give me that impression. Tate and Randy, on the other hand,"

"Those two are idiots."

"That they are, but they're also two idiots who can implicate you."

"What are you going to do?"

I popped the rest of my waffle cone into my mouth, wiped my hands, and tossed the napkin onto the table.

"I'm gonna make him an offer he can't refuse," I said mimicking Don Corleone in The Godfather.

After dropping Latrice and her children off at their apartment, I called Clive. It was time to see what level of shit Kincade had gotten into over the years. My Spidey senses tingled every time I met the guy, and it wasn't just because he was a sleaze-ball. That man was up to something, and I planned to find out exactly what it was. I figured it would take his accountant and attorney at least a few days to get their ducks in a row before going after Latrice.

Clive picked up on the second ring.

"Hey, Ms. D. What up?"

"Clive, get me everything you can find on Tom Kincade. And I mean everything. If he so much as paid a bill late, I want to know every detail."

"Sure thing, Ms. D."

Chapter Eighteen

TUESDAY MORNING, I was finally able to get an appointment with Detective Halliday and his partner, Detective McDonough. Both had recently transferred from Homicide to the Field Investigation Unit and Omaha was keeping them busy. I met with them downtown.

"All right, Jackson, you said you have something on a suicide that's already been ruled a suicide. The Libby Walker case is closed."

I sat across from them at a small conference table in a nondescript space, one side of which was lined with glass walls. Halliday bounced the tip of a pen up and down on the table. McDonough, toothpick dangling from the corner of his mouth, waited for me to answer. Halliday was at least sixty years old, and McDonough wasn't much younger.

"I found this," I slid the bag containing the small metal piece across the table to Detective Halliday. He set down his pen to pick it up. "In Libby Walker's apartment. Actually, her sister discovered it while I was there."

"What is it?" Detective McDonough asked.

"Tracer's people say it's used to collect and transmit data."

Detective Halliday examined both sides, turning it over a few times before handing it off to Detective McDonough.

"What kind of data?" McDonough asked.

"Tracer believes it transmits high-frequency sounds."

"What? Like what a dog can hear?" Halliday asked.

"Something like that. It's more along the lines of that Mosquito device." Several law enforcement agencies were familiar with it, and some had already begun using it to control crowds. "I'm guessing this showed up after you and your people left the scene."

Detective Halliday nodded like he was taking it all in.

"This doesn't necessarily change anything, Jackson," McDonough said. "But we'll look into it."

"That's all I can ask," I said, then stood to leave.

"How's your dog?" McDonough asked as we stepped into the main office area. "We heard he took one for you."

"Godfrey is still with the vet, but my vet says he'll be okay. Almost ready to come home."

"Yeah," McDonough scratched his neck. "He's a good dog. I knew his partner way back. Glad to know Godfrey found a home."

"CLIVE? WHAT IS IT? Do you have something for me on Kincade?"

I'd just left my meeting with the detectives and was on my way to the Jeep when my phone rang.

"No, but I found Anna Summers." He waited a few beats too long.

"Okay, why the drama? Where is she?"

"Dead."

I stopped walking. "What? How? When?"

"Nearest I can tell, it was about a year before Castle had his affair with CeCe Stiles."

"How'd she die?"

"Coroner ruled it a suicide."

"What do you know about her? Was she taking any medications?"

"I don't know. I just started digging into this."

It can't be a coincidence that two of the women he had an affair with committed suicide. That's either incredibly shitty luck, or he targets troubled young women. If I was the gambling sort, I'd bet on the latter.

"Keep searching. Oh, and get me something, anything, on Kincade."

"I got you covered, Ms. D. I'm all over it."

Chapter Nineteen

I DECIDED IT WAS TIME to come clean with Patricia Castle. Chances were Rick Castle didn't tell her anything about our meeting the other day. So far, I knew Matt Anderson told her about the affairs with CeCe Stiles and Anna Summers, but she supposedly didn't know about Libby Walker. It was time to see what Patricia Castle really thought about her husband's inability to keep his pants up.

She was teaching classes today, so I drove to the campus. After talking with someone to get directions, I found her class and parked myself outside, leaning against a wall. Ten minutes later students emerged. I waited for the traffic to disperse and entered the classroom from the back. Patricia Castle stood at the front reviewing papers.

"Mrs. Castle?"

She looked up, surprised to see me. I handed her my card. Her eyes scanned it and then widened.

"I'm sorry about lying to you when we met. Sometimes it's a necessary part of the job."

"What's this really about, then?" She set a handful of papers back onto the desk in front of her.

"You hired a gentleman by the name of Matt Anderson to investigate your husband."

"Yes, so?"

"I've been doing this work a long time, Mrs. Castle. When a spouse does that, it's usually because they suspect their partner is having an affair. And in your case, you discovered that he's had at least three."

Blood drained from her face. Maybe she didn't know about Libby Walker.

"Three?"

"Anna Summers, CeCe Stiles, and Libby Walker."

"Libby Walker? That girl who committed suicide?"

"She was pregnant."

I waited for that to sink in. Her fingers drifted to a charm on her necklace. She fiddled with it, flipping it between her fingers.

"I — I hired Mr. Anderson, and he told me about Stiles and Summers. That's true. But I know nothing about Libby Walker. She was pregnant? Are you sure Rick was seeing her? Are you saying the baby was his?"

"I can't say that for certain. But yes, he had been seeing her until about a month before her suicide."

She pulled out a chair and sat.

"What am I supposed to do with this information? Wait, you're here because you think Rick had something to do with that girl's death." The realization sent a rush of blood to her face. "There's no way Rick — yes, he's a shit for having a few flings, but to kill someone? No, no, that doesn't make any sense. He — we would lose everything." She nestled her forehead in her left hand and rubbed her temples.

"Anna Summers also committed suicide."

She looked up at me, her jawline tightened. "What are you saying?"

"That's a strange coincidence, don't you think?"

Rolling her chair back, she stood and braced her hands on the table for support. "Get out!"

Starting the engine, I pulled out of my parking spot and eased into a line of traffic funneling toward the campus exit. All things considered, I thought the meeting with Patricia went great. I'd let her mull our conversation over for a few days, then check back in on her. Now, though, I needed to deal with Kincade.

KINCADE WAS IN HIS usual spot in the back office when I knocked on the door. Without looking up, he growled, "What?"

"We need to talk," I said and stepped inside, closing the door partway.

"Good, I was just about to call you. What else do you have for me on Latrice?"

"You know what Mr. Kincade? The internet is an amazing resource, especially in the hands of skilled researchers."

"What are you talking about?"

I removed a small manila envelope from my satchel and rested it on the desk along with my camera. He looked at the envelope and then back at me.

"What's this crap?"

"Open it."

He unfastened the metal clasp, reached in, and pulled out an SD card.

"Would you like to see what I found?" Placing the card into my camera, I tapped a button and turned it so he could view the images. "Oh, wait, I especially like this. How did you get into that position?"

Tom Kincade's usually chalk-white skin flushed with patches of red, his hands balled into fists, and his knuckles turned white.

"Wait, there's more. You're going to love this." I switched to video mode. "Honestly, you're more limber than I thought."

"What the hell is this? What are you trying to do?" He slammed his hands onto the desk and stood. His chair smacked the table behind him, and the coffee he'd been drinking spilled. I scooped up my camera.

"Here's the deal, Kincade. You're going to let Latrice, Tate, and Randy go. You're not firing them. Call it a layoff if you want."

"Or, what? This isn't anything!" He waved off the camera as though he could dismiss its existence.

"If I understand this little arrangement correctly, and to be clear, I'm usually right about these things, this woman," I pointed to the one in the video, then flipped through a few images, "And this one here, are both prostitutes. If I recall, solicitation still is a crime in Nebraska. Oh, and then there's pandering."

"You're a piece of shit, Jackson!"

"It gets better." I pointed to the screen. "That girl is maybe sixteen years old. Do you know what that means?" Kincade stared at me in disbelief. "Go ahead, ask me. You know you want to know." I waited a few seconds for effect. "No? I'll tell you, anyway. That's a class IV felony. With your other two convictions," His expression went from disbelief to confusion and back again. "Oh, yeah, I know about those, too. Did you know that a Class IV felony carries up to a five-year sentence and you could pay a ten thousand dollar fine? That combined with a pandering charge, and wow, when I read about that, I said to myself, 'Jackson, I wonder if Kincade knows that?'"

He grabbed for the camera.

"Ah, ah, ah." I said, finger wagging like I was scolding a child. "This is mine. Unless,"

"Fine!"

"Fine, what?"

"I'll drop it."

"I'm going to need that in writing. You can use that notepad behind you. It would be really nice if you could include some sort of recommendation for them, too. You know, for their job search."

He mumbled something and started writing.

"You're going to need two sheets per person."

I was feeling a rush after my chat with Tom Kincade. The letters were safely tucked away in my satchel, and I had given him the SD card. What he neglected to ask, and I failed to mention, was that I had a copy of every single image and video. The Clifton StrengthFinder tagged me as input and intellection, among other things. Gathering data and holding it for later use is in my DNA. Kincade was exactly the kind of guy I needed to keep information about. When I arrived home, I made copies of the letters, and placed them into my office safe. I'd get the originals to Latrice, Tate, and Randy tomorrow.

The message light on my phone blinked incessantly. I keyed in the passcode and heard Dr. Roberts' smooth voice letting me know that I could pick up Godfrey tonight before five-thirty. It was already four-forty-five, but if I hurried, I'd make it.

Chapter Twenty

IN THE MORNING, MY mind was awake before my body wanted to move. I made a mental list of the loose ends that still needed following up on for both the Kincade and Walker cases. Rather than track down Tate and Randy, I'd pop the letters from Kincade into the mail. To be honest, talking with those two idiots wasn't high on my psychological needs list. I also wanted to track down Anna Summers' family. Talking with them might give me more insights into Rick Castle. There was more to his relationship with Libby Walker than what he wanted me to believe. I just didn't know what that was, yet. Then there was Latrice. Getting the letters to her was a top priority this morning. I didn't want her stewing over something that was resolved. It's hard enough being a single parent and then you toss shitty boss into the mix, and a downward spiral happens with little effort.

Finally satisfied with the day's plan, I kicked off the blanket and got out of bed. After a quick shower, I slid into a pair of black jeans, an emerald green ribbed, mock turtleneck, and a pair of flame-printed Converse. Sunlight crept through the window shades, but I knew that wasn't a sign of warmth outside, so I checked the weather app on my phone. Mid-fifties wasn't so bad for a fall day. I made my way downstairs to the kitchen.

Godfrey, still asleep on his bed, made me feel the warmth that seeing the sun lacked. The house was a morgue without him. I reached down to pet his head, and he stirred, then began to stretch. Grabbing a small piece of chicken from the fridge, I set it in front of Godfrey's nose. In mere seconds, it disappeared. He was going to be fine. I let him outside before making my breakfast and cursed myself for forgetting to buy bagels. I settled on a bowl of cereal and Breakfast Serenade tea instead.

It was seven o'clock, and I figured that Latrice was probably up and wrangling her kids, so I gave her a quick call. I planned to head over there around eight-thirty. That would give her time to drop her rug rats at their schools.

Godfrey scratched at the door and then followed me to my office.

"I've got to get going pretty soon, Godfrey." He sat at the entrance of my office, his big brown eyes staring up at me. I knelt and wrapped my arms around his thick neck. "Thanks for having my back, Godfrey." He ambled back to his bed in the kitchen.

LATRICE'S APARTMENT complex surrounded an internal courtyard with a fenced pool and playground just outside of that. Benches lined the perimeter of the playground and a few picnic tables, accompanied by grills, hid beneath a large canopy. The pool had been drained for the season and a padlock held the gate closed. A few moms, with toddlers strapped into swings, engaged in the latest inter-complex gossip.

I waved to Latrice, who was seated at a picnic table away from the other women. When I reached the table, I pulled my satchel over my head before sitting across from her. Setting my bag onto the table, I removed the letters and handed them to Latrice.

"What's this?"

"Your insurance policy."

She opened them. As she began reading the second one, a tear slid down her cheek, and she swept it away with her shirtsleeve.

"I don't understand. Why would he do this?"

"The important thing here is that he did, and you can move on without looking over your shoulder. Clean slate."

"But how did you convince him?"

"It's what I do, Latrice. Everybody has secrets, and I'm really good at finding out what they are. Keep that," I pointed to the letter forgiving her debt to Kincade, "In a safe place. I had him write the letter of recommendation for good measure. It doesn't mean employers won't call him, but legally he's not allowed to give them anything but your employment dates."

"Yeah, but there's always ways,"

"I know, but in this case, he's not going to take advantage of those. Dates of employment, and nothing else. That's the deal, and he knows better than to screw up."

She set them onto the table in front of her and placed a travel mug on top.

"People don't fuck with you, do they?"

"I don't know about that. Some try."

"You look like you're in good shape. Is that from special private investigator training or something?"

"Nah. I practice Hapkido and jiujitsu a few times a week, and sometimes I teach a class."

"Now, I know nobody messes with you! Shit, girl, you're like the Black Widow, only not as pale." She laughed and her hands played with the lid on her mug.

"Maybe that's what I need to do. Ever since Malcolm passed, it's just been so hard. Every damn day is a struggle."

"Losing someone is never easy."

"People mean well, but then some — they just start pushing my buttons. The manager here is after me about the rent - like I suddenly got a windfall of money. Malcolm didn't have much life insurance, just a small policy. I used it to set up education funds for the kids."

"That seems like a good use for the money."

"Yeah, I figured I'd be working, so day-to-day crap would get taken care of, but with the rent increase, I'm just done, ya know?"

"Have you checked into College of St. Mary, yet?"

"Called yesterday. I have an appointment tomorrow. Thanks for hooking me up with that." She sipped from her mug. "How'd you get into what you do?"

"My father was in military intelligence. It just sort of rubbed off, and I studied criminal justice and psychology. Tracer International, they're an international security firm, recruited me when I went to UNL."

"You carry?"

"All the time, but my preference is to talk my way out of shit. If I can't, then I might throw down. Guns are a last resort in my world. Way too permanent and the paperwork after sucks."

"I did okay in school. My mom's a CNA. She kept telling me nursing was the future 'cause there's always a demand for them."

I nodded my head, "She's right about that. Personally, I could never do it, but if you've got the stomach for it, then it's a good field."

"Where do you teach those classes?"

"Depends. Sometimes the Y on Maple, sometimes Master Simmons place." I knew she'd know where that was. Her place was within walking distance of the Benson business district. "Might be one coming up, soon. You interested?"

"How much does it cost?"

"It's free for women and children eighteen to about six-years-old. Some of the younger kids aren't ready and can't handle themselves, but your kids would probably take to it. "Lasts a week." I reached into a side pocket in my bag, my fingers fumbling to find cards for the dojang, and then handed one to her. "The kids train in a separate area. You need to call to sign up and spots usually fill up quick."

She examined the card, then put it into her back pocket.

"Does it hurt?"

"Does what hurt?"

"Getting hit."

"The idea is to not get hit, but yeah, it stings. Wrist locks hurt for as long as you apply force, but most people don't feel it much after you release them. Our focus for the week is self-defense you can actually use, and that includes a lot of emphasis on situational awareness."

"Maybe I'll check into it. I gotta find someone to watch the baby, and hopefully I'll be starting classes soon." A smile spread across her face. Latrice's deep blue eyes reminded me of my grandmother's.

"How long before I get as good as you?" The smile remained.

"That depends on you. I started training when I was a kid. My parents owned a dojang, but even before that, I was on the mats. The thing about Hapkido is anyone can learn techniques and get good at executing them in a relatively brief time. Jiujitsu is a little different — takes more time. What some people don't realize is that it all needs to become muscle memory. But you can practice situational awareness everywhere." I scanned the area, then said, "How many people are back here with us?" Latrice started to turn her head to look. "Don't look. What do you remember and what have you noticed since we sat down?"

"Shit, I don't know, maybe three ladies with their kids."

"Four. One has two. Two have one, and the last woman is just hanging out. There's also a man that showed up about ten minutes ago. He's been checking things out in the maintenance shed. He snubbed a cigarette on the building before he went inside. Tall, thin, dark-skinned, wearing a low-profile baseball cap."

"Okay, I get your point. Notice more, talk less."

"Pretty much."

AFTER A LITTLE DIGGING, I learned that Anna Summers left UNO and transferred to Wayne State about two hours northwest of Omaha. It was during her time there that she committed suicide, but it was only a short time after having moved. Her mother lived in Ralston, and her father remarried and lives in Florida. I called Mrs. Summers to see if she'd be willing to talk with me. Our meeting was set for six o'clock at her house.

Having caught up on all my invoicing and a few bills, I didn't have anything pressing to do. The house still was in a state of disarray, but I wasn't motivated to do much about that. I grabbed my bow and headed outside to the backyard to practice. Shooting is meditative in a way that actual meditation never is. My stance and shoulders relax just before taking a deep breath. I center, aim, and release the arrow, leaving the fingers of my right hand resting atop my shoulder. Then I do it all again. I've been known to practice for an hour or more. Sometimes if I'm not feeling settled enough after an hour, then I pull out my throwing knives. Today, though, I didn't have an hour. I wanted to check in with Clive about the building and his proposal, then get something to eat before meeting Mrs. Summers.

Thirty minutes passed and I returned my bow to its case, then went inside to call Clive. Godfrey was out cold on his bed. Since I didn't plan on being back too late, I left him alone and made sure he had plenty of water. I'd get him something to eat when I returned home.

Clive's phone went to voicemail. I hate leaving messages, so I hung up knowing that when he saw it was me, he'd call back. On my way out the door, I slung the strap of my bag over my head and walked down the stairs to my Jeep. Then my phone rang. Fumbling for it in my bag, I dropped my keys before answering.

"Dez Jackson."

"What's up, Ms. D?"

"Where are you?"

"My office, as usual."

"You eat, yet?"

"I could get a bite."

Fifteen minutes later, I pulled into the parking lot of Do Space and saw Clive standing near the entrance talking with a group of three young college-age women. They wore pink and green giving away their allegiance to the Alpha Kappa Alpha sorority. I had no clue what he was saying to them, but he had the girls smiling and giggling.

To give him a little more time to work his magic, I swung the Jeep around the lot and pulled into a spot facing the building and to the right of the door. I honked once. He looked over, gave a quick head nod, then said goodbye to the ladies.

Climbing into the passenger seat, he said, "What we eaten'?"

"Zio's?"

"Nah, I had pizza last night. What about Chinese?"

I pointed the Jeep in the direction of a buffet just west on Dodge. The five-minute ride there was quiet. Clive's head bobbed as he listened to music through his ear buds. We entered the restaurant and had our pick of places to sit. I guessed the place wasn't a hotspot for the after-work crowd, but I had no complaints. As we walked past the buffet, I examined the offerings. My stomach did a happy dance when my eyes landed on fried donuts sprinkled in sugar. I promised myself I'd get that last. We didn't bother to sit, just placed our bags down, and went back to the buffet to load up our plates. When we returned to our table, they had placed water glasses onto it.

"Let's talk about Detrick's — your building."

He peered up at me from his plate, mouth filled with a half-eaten egg roll.

"If we're going to be partners, then it has to be a straight-up, backed by paper arrangement. I'm willing to go in initially with an eighty-twenty split with you getting the twenty. After you're positioned to take care of at least fifty percent of the bills, then we can reassess the arrangement."

"Sixty-forty."

I'd almost forgotten I wasn't dealing with a newbie.

"Seventy-five, twenty-five."

"You know I'll be managing the place, getting the tenants and what not. That's worth at least thirty."

I finished my food and pushed the plate to the side. My eyes wandered to the buffet and the pile of donuts.

"Fine, seventy-thirty, but we're going to have a few rules in place."

"Rules? Like what?"

"How about no setting the place up for unauthorized parties?"

"We could get a liquor license."

I balled up my napkin and threw it at him. It smacked him in the face and fell to his empty plate.

"It was just a suggestion!"

I DROPPED CLIVE AT a friend's house and made my way through five o'clock traffic to Summers' house in Ralston. She lived on a tree-lined street filled with houses built in the eighties. I parked along the street outside her pale blue house. A neatly trimmed lawn and path of boxwood bushes guided me to the front door. I laughed at myself for knowing the name of the bushes. She opened the door before I knocked.

"Ms. Jackson? Please come in."

"Thank you."

The front door opened into a split entry; one set of stairs led to the basement and another to the main floor. I followed her up to a quaint living room furnished with a couch, two Lazy Boy recliners, a few side tables, and a large flat-screen TV mounted to a wall. The kitchen was just beyond the living room. To my left, there were four doors, one of which likely led to a bathroom.

"Can I get you something to drink? Water?"

"No, thank you."

"Please, make yourself comfortable." She gestured to the couch and then sat in one of the recliners. "You said this is about Anna?"

"Yes, I was wondering if you could tell me more about her, "

"Suicide?"

"More specifically about who found her, what was there, anything you can recall would be a great help."

"What's this about? Why do you need to know about my Anna?"

"I'm working a case that might be related."

"Related? How?"

"It's a long shot, really, but I'm trying to see if there are any similarities between Anna's case and mine."

"I don't know what to tell you. I wasn't there when it happened. Her roommate found her."

"Was Anna involved with anyone at the time?"

Mrs. Summers considered this for a minute. Her eyes focused past me to a wall near the TV filled with family pictures.

"She had been seeing someone, but she broke it off. That was about the time she transferred to Wayne. I never met him."

"Do you recall his name?"

She shook her head. "Anna had become very private when she went to college. I suppose that's normal for most kids these days. They get out of their parent's home and want to live their own lives."

"Do you know how long she had been seeing whoever it was?"

"Six, maybe eight months? When it ended, she seemed relieved."

"Was Anna taking any medications? Anything at all?"

"I'm sure she was taking birth control, but aside from that, I don't believe so."

"Was anything found with her?"

"No." She paused. "She had a watch on, but it was broken. It was a beautiful watch. I'd asked her where she found it, but she never said. We were busy clearing things out for a garage sale that day."

"You wouldn't happen to still have the watch, would you?"

"Yes, I do. Give me one sec." She left the room, went down the hall, and disappeared into one of the rooms. I occupied myself with a quick scan of the living room, making note of who was in the pictures. Anna had long, strawberry-blonde curly hair. She was only a few inches taller than her mother. By my calculations, that put her at about five feet five inches tall. She looked healthy and fit.

"Here you are." Mrs. Summers handed the watch to me. The front glass was broken. I examined the strap and the back of the watch, turning it over a few times in my hands.

"What's this?" I asked, pointing to what looked like a Roman numeral on its back.

"Huh. I never noticed that before."

"Do you mind if I take a picture?"

She shrugged, and said, "Not at all. If you think it'll help you in some way."

"So, do you think the person she was seeing gave her this watch?"

She nodded. "Yes, I do. That's the only reason I think she didn't want to tell me anything about it. I got the impression that whoever she had been seeing was older than her. She knew I wouldn't approve, so she just kept it to herself. She wasn't like that during high school. I met all of her boyfriends then."

"But you're sure she ended the relationship before transferring to Wayne?"

"Yes, I'm fairly certain of that."

"Did you notice anything strange about her behavior before she transferred?"

"She was starting to get; I don't know the best way to describe it." She smoothed her pant legs. "Paranoid."

"How do you mean?"

"It was little things, things most people who didn't really know her wouldn't have noticed. And everything needed to be just so. She used to live in complete clutter and chaos. Her room always looked like the aftermath of a tornado. Her apartment was, too. But one day I popped over to give her some laundry she'd left here, and her apartment was spotless."

"Maybe she was just growing up."

"Maybe, but I think it had more to do with whoever she was seeing. I think he was I don't know — controlling her. An older man involved with a younger woman — the men tend to be like that."

"You sound like you're speaking from experience."

"My ex married a woman twenty years younger than he is. That's exactly what their relationship is like. It's disgusting."

"But you don't know why Anna ended the relationship?"

"No. All she said was that she planned to transfer because she wanted a change of scenery. By then she seemed better, like she was thinking clearly. It didn't make sense that she'd kill herself."

"And it was ruled a suicide?"

"Yes. There wasn't any sort of investigation to speak of. Why? Do you think something else happened?" She seemed hopeful.

"I don't know. It's probably nothing. I'm just dotting the i's and crossing the t's, you know." I checked the time on my phone. "Wow, I didn't mean to take up so much of your time." I stood to leave. "Thank you. You've been a great help."

"If you find out anything more about Anna, please tell me." She walked me to the door.

"I will. Thank you again for your time, Mrs. Summers. You've been very helpful."

Chapter Twenty-One

SUSIE WALKER SAT AT a table near the door as I entered Scooters Coffeehouse. I always wondered why the owners set up near a Starbuck's, and figured Scooters wouldn't make it, but here it was. Coffee drinkers are loyal to specific companies, I guess. I smiled at Susie and gestured that I was going to order something.

"Welcome to Scooters." The barista, who was probably in her twenties, was way too enthusiastic for this hour of the morning. Susie had to be at work at seven o'clock, so I agreed to meet her at six-fifteen. I ordered a tea and a muffin, then returned to Susie's table.

"Thanks for meeting me." I pulled out the chair, setting my satchel on one of the unoccupied ones. "I met a woman last night whose daughter committed suicide."

"Oh, my God. That's horrible."

"It was more than a year ago. Here's the thing, though, the girl — her name was Anna, she also had a relationship with a man who gave her a watch." I pulled the pictures up on my phone. "This watch."

Susie examined the two images I'd taken.

"Does this look anything like the one Libby wore?"

"What's this on the back? A number?"

"I'm not sure if it means anything. Did her watch look like this one?"

"Yeah, it did. I don't know if it had anything like this on the back of it, though," she said, handing my phone to me. "So, you think that Rick Castle was seeing this other girl, Anna?"

"Her mother didn't know the man's name, but I know that Anna Summers was seeing Rick Castle at some point. It can't be a coincidence."

"See, there's something wrong with that man!"

"Because of a watch? It might just be some sort of fetish-like thing he does."

"Like a serial killer." She said, almost inaudibly.

I leaned closer, my elbows resting on the table. "Susie, don't get carried away. All we know for sure is that Rick Castle was seeing three young women over the course of the past two years. Each of whom was somewhere between nineteen and twenty-one when he began relationships with them."

"And that he gives them all watches."

"Apparently. The question is, why? Maybe it's some emotional attachment thing. Maybe he likes time pieces. Maybe the watches don't mean anything. They could have been gifts and nothing more. We don't know."

In the back of my mind, one thing nagged at me. Why did Rick Castle go to Stiles' apartment that day and take the watch? If it was just a gift, why take it back? Was he being spiteful because she dumped him? That seems far-fetched considering how he described his relationship with Libby. He called that a fling. Wouldn't it follow that he viewed all his indiscretions that way?

"Rick Castle said that he ended his relationship with your sister and that it was a fling."

Susie had been absentmindedly nibbling at a muffin of her own. "No, that's not true. Libby would have told me. They were still seeing each other when he was trying to convince her to have an abortion. What else do you know about Anna?"

"She broke off the relationship and then transferred to Wayne State. Her mother mentioned that Anna had changed while she was seeing Castle — almost like she had OCD and mild paranoia, but her mother thought Anna was getting back to normal. The other woman he was seeing is CeCe Stiles. She also stopped seeing him. The strange thing is, he gave her a watch, but then he took it back."

"I'm telling you, Dez. It's just like you always read about. The crazy killer always collects things from their victims. Like they're keeping a souvenir or something." She took a few sips from her coffee. "Only this time, he's giving them things and taking them back. Maybe he just couldn't get to Anna."

I couldn't see Rick Castle as a serial killer, but then no one saw Bundy that way, either. Still, it didn't make much sense. My gut told me he was a manipulative, egotistical, somewhat narcissistic person. He craved attention and loved the spotlight. And he liked to be in control of the people around him, especially the females from what I determined so far.

"Oh, crap! I need to get to work!" Susie grabbed her phone and stood so quickly her chair almost tipped over and hit the floor. Grabbing the back of it, she said, "I told you there's something wrong with that man, and he did something to Libby, just like he probably did something to that girl Anna. And if the other one hadn't gotten away from him, she'd probably be dead, too."

"We need more than feelings to go to the police. They won't take another look without something damned compelling."

"That's why you've got to keep looking. This isn't just about Libby anymore." She took a last sip of her coffee, then tossed the cup into the garbage. "I really appreciate your help, Dez. No one else would have even bothered." The weak smile on her face conveyed profound loss masked as hope.

"I'll keep looking, Susie. If there's anything to it, I'll find out what it is."

I watched her disappear into the parking lot, get into a grey Honda, and pull into early morning traffic. Lucky for her, HyVee was only a few minutes away.

At this point, I wasn't entirely sure where to go next. Castle wouldn't tell me anything new. If I approached him about Anna or CeCe, the most I could hope was that he'd confirm the relationships. Then again, I should let him do that and ask about those watches. The more I considered it, the more I realized that I'd like to see his reaction about the watches.

My marching orders decided, I finished the tea, tossed everything into the garbage bin, and headed outside to my Jeep.

CASTLE'S ASSISTANT, still believing that I was writing an article about him, told me where I could find him this afternoon. He liked eating lunch at the same place several times each week, and today was my lucky day. She said I'd find him at the Salty Sisters Diner about a block down and a jog to the east. I'd never been there, but the name intrigued me.

The crumbling brick facade of the Salty Sisters Diner had been all white. Now bits of coppery red brick peeked through the paint in several spots. As I entered, the sweet aroma of maple syrup made my stomach rumble and I had to remind myself that I wasn't here to eat. A handful of patrons sat at a breakfast bar that stretched the length of the space, and most of the tables were occupied. A large wall-mounted clock made of utensils told me that the lunch rush would end soon. A sign near the door read, "What are you waiting for? Sit down." My eyes scanned the room and found Rick Castle seated alone in a booth near windows with a bad view.

"Mind if I join you?" I smiled and set my bag onto the seat opposite his.

"Not at all, Ms. Jackson." He wiped his hands and set his napkin onto the table to his left. "I was just leaving."

"Before you go, I was hoping you could help me understand something."

He pushed back, clasped his hands together, and allowed them to rest atop the table. Castle inhaled deeply before answering.

"What is it now, Ms. Jackson? I've already told you everything you need to know about my relationship with Libby."

"Maybe yes, maybe no."

"I don't have time for games. Get to the point."

I scrolled through the images on my phone until I found the watch and set it on the table between us.

"Does this look familiar to you?"

He glanced down, then his eyes met mine. His brows squeezed together, and his jawline tightened. Castle leaned forward, one hand covering the fist of the other.

"I'm just curious if you know what happened to it. Susie mentioned that Libby wore this watch and never took it off, but it wasn't on her when Susie found her."

"What are you playing at?"

"I don't know what you mean. This is the watch you gave to Libby Walker, isn't it?" I slid the image to the view of the backside showing the Roman numeral, then flipped between the two images a few times. "It looks like an expensive gift for someone who was just a fling, don't ya think?"

"The relationship ended, Ms. Jackson. I already explained that to you, and that is all I will say on the matter." He got up.

"Oh, wait." I made a show of examining the images. "This isn't Libby Walker's watch. This one belonged to Anna Summers," I said, tilting my head to look up at him. He slid back into the bench seat. "She committed suicide, too. That's a little strange, right? I mean, what are the odds that two women, both of whom had a relationship with you, committed suicide?"

"I had nothing to do with Anna Summers' death. Our relationship was over long before that."

"Are ya sure? I mean, her mother seemed to think differently."

"Ms. Jackson, you don't know what you're talking about. Now, if you will excuse me, I have more pressing work to attend to, and this," he gestured at my phone, "has nothing to do with me or my wife."

That was interesting. I hadn't brought up his wife.

"You know what's even stranger than this?" I waited a beat. When he didn't say anything, I continued. "I met a woman named CeCe Stiles a few days ago, and she said that you and she also had a relationship. Let me guess, that was just a fling, too. What is that, three so far? Your wife really is a patient woman. If I were her, I would have kicked your sorry ass to the curb long before now."

Castle stood to leave, grabbing his suit jacket from a hook on the side of the bench. Slinging it over his arm, he said, "You and I have nothing further to discuss."

"Maybe." I smiled and watched as he turned to walk away.

DETECTIVE HALLIDAY and his partner frequented a place called O'Malley's on east Center Street. It was a laid-back neighborhood pub that back in the day would have been smoke-filled and for whites only. There wouldn't have been signs to that effect, but everyone just knew. Now it was primarily a cop-only kind of place. The owner, Pete O'Malley, didn't seem too concerned about that. I spied him leaning against the back bar at the far end, arms crossed, laughing at something a cop seated in front of him said. O'Malley was a third-generation pub owner, and he looked just like the O'Malley men before him — red hair cropped short, pale skin, and a lean, but muscular build. At just over six feet tall, he towered over me, but I'd gotten him to the mat on more than one occasion.

It was six-thirty and no table or chair remained empty. Several off-duty officers gathered around the bar swapping stories about arrests, and who did what, when. I ordered a gin & tonic. The bartender set it in front of me and said, "On the house." Leaning forward, I searched the length of the bar and my eyes settled on Pete. He gave me a slight head nod. I returned the sentiment, then pushed off to find Halliday and McDonough.

I found them in the back playing doubles in what looked like a heated battle for the eight-ball. One of their opponents was up. Their last ball was snugged up against the eight-ball dead center at the opposite end of the table, and a little more than a foot from the rail. I set my drink onto a high-top table to watch. In my experience, there weren't many amateurs who could clean their ball from the eight-ball without scratching. The best this guy could hope for was to nestle the cue ball close to them both, but he had to hit his ball first. It's not the play I'd make, but then I'm not an amateur. The sound of the tip connecting with the cue ball told me all I needed to know. The eight-ball sunk, Halliday and McDonough cheered, and the other two handed over a twenty. It got me thinking that maybe I should play here once in a while, but stripping a few of Omaha's finest of their hard-earned money wouldn't be good for business.

Halliday noticed me first. "What are you doing here, Jackson?"

"I was in the neighborhood and got thirsty."

"Phewww, I'm callin' bullshit on that one." He sat on the stool across from me and rested his stick against the wall while McDonough got ready to break. "What do you want?"

"Why do you always assume I want something?"

He stared at me without saying a word and waited.

"I don't want anything, exactly. It's more like I have some more information to share about the Libby Walker case."

"There isn't a Libby Walker case. It's closed."

"But you have to admit that metal piece is interesting, especially given what I know now."

"Get on with it, Jackson. My shift is over and I'm trying to wind down."

"I talked with a man named Rick Castle today."

"Yeah, yeah. And this is important, how?"

"He was dating Libby Walker around the time of her supposed suicide."

"It was a suicide, Jackson. Supposed doesn't enter the equation."

"Just hear me out."

He took a long pull from his bear, then set it down. "I'm all ears."

"They stopped seeing each other not long before she died. And you already know she was pregnant."

"Get to the point, Jackson."

"It was Castle's baby. He insists that she didn't want it and that he planned to give her money for an abortion. The problem is that Libby's sister says that Libby was happy about the baby and planned to keep it."

"Okay, and?"

"Castle is married with a family of his own. He's a hotshot researcher at SMT Tech."

"The outfit that does all that defense contracting."

"Exactly. His specialty is sound. Now, I'm not going to pretend that I understand what the hell he does, but something doesn't feel right." I pulled up the pictures of the watch on my phone. "This belonged to a young woman Castle dated about a year ago. She committed suicide, too. Her name was Anna Summers. Castle also was dating another woman named CeCe Stiles, and she had a watch very similar to this one, but Castle took it back from her when she broke things off. Susie Walker said Libby also had a watch, but that it was missing when she found her sister. According to Susie, Libby never took off her watch."

"So, the man has a fetish for watches."

"You see that number on the back?"

He picked up my phone for a closer inspection.

"I'm betting CeCe's and Libby's watches had numbers on them. Like he's tracking them."

"Jackson, all you have is possibly some circumstantial evidence. Why am I telling you this? You know how this shit works. It's not enough for me to reopen a suicide case."

"Okay, but,"

"But nothing. You're wasting my time and I'm trying to relax."

"What if that metal piece and the watches are connected somehow?"

"And do what?"

"I don't know."

"Exactly. You don't know. Come back to me when you do. Until then, grab a stick or move out."

"You don't want her to do that." I turned to see Pete O'Malley standing a few feet from me, his blue-green eyes dancing with his broad smile. "She'll take everything you have including your unborn children."

"That's not entirely accurate," I said, looking at Pete and then back to Halliday. "I don't want kids."

"Be that as it may, come back when you've got something I can use. Until then, we don't need to see each other."

"So harsh. I thought you liked me," I said smiling, and stood, gulped down the rest of my drink, and set the glass back down. "I'll be in touch."

Chapter Twenty-Two

"HAITHEM, THANKS FOR meeting me." After my chat with Detective Halliday yesterday, I decided I needed more answers about that little metal device and the watches. There had to be a connection, but I had no clue what it might be. The only people I knew smart enough to figure it out worked for Tracer, so I called Haithem.

Haithem's svelte body looked even more enticing than usual as he dabbed sweat from his face, neck, and shoulders.

"Good work out?"

"Not bad. I haven't had any challenging training partners of late. Perhaps you should visit more often." He smiled and sat in the chair next to mine, resting the hand towel across his left thigh. "I was able to get in a decent run, but my exercise regimen isn't what brought you all the way to Lincoln on what's shaping up to be a beautiful autumn day."

Haithem's gaze shifted to the large floor-to-ceiling windows in the lobby. The leaves on the trees lining the pathway to the fitness center dazzled with shades and hues of red, orange, and yellow. A breeze shuffled the limbs, releasing several leaves onto the sidewalk and browning grass below.

"I've been thinking more about that metal piece. Take a look at this." I handed Haithem my phone. "That watch belonged to another woman who also committed suicide. So far, I know my guy gave a watch like this to two other women."

"Tell me they haven't all killed themselves," Haithem said as he examined the two images.

"One hasn't."

"Are you concerned that she might?" He looked up from the images.

"No, I think she got away from him just in time, but I'm not exactly sure what she got away from."

"But you think it has something to do with this watch and the metal device."

I nodded. "I just don't know how either connect or even if they actually do connect."

"Can you get me this watch?"

"Possibly. The girl's mother still has it."

"Let's start there. If there's anything to it, we'll find it."

On my way back to Omaha, I called Mrs. Summers to arrange a time to retrieve the watch. She had plans, but said she'd be available after three o'clock. That gave me plenty of time to get back to Omaha, get in a quick at-home workout, clean-up, get lunch, and do a few odds and ends.

When I arrived home, I changed into yoga pants and an UnderArmor long-sleeve running shirt — not because I planned to run, that would only happen if a lion was chasing me — but because that's more comfortable to workout in than jeans and T-shirt. To be honest, running on a treadmill occasionally isn't awful, but sucking in frosty air outside, or hot air for that matter, is only worth doing in an emergency.

Godfrey hid beneath the deck behind a set of stacked chairs the minute he saw my weapons bag. I removed my quiver from over my shoulder, set down my bow case, and placed the bag onto the ground to unpack my knives.

"What are you worried about?" His ears perked up, and he tilted his head as if to say, "Who, me?"

After a few rounds with my knives and arrows, I packed things up and headed inside to the basement for a heavy bag workout. Godfrey, feeling braver, or maybe safer, followed but opted to crash on his bed in the kitchen. By the time I finished, it was one-thirty, and I was in desperate need of a shower. As I resurfaced from my dungeon, I saw Godfrey perched in front of his food dish. He looked from it to me and back again.

"It's not time to eat, Godfrey." He whined. "No, Dr. Roberts told me not to over feed you." He barked. "Okay, you win, but I'm only giving you a snack."

I kept Godfrey's treats above the refrigerator because I learned early that he'd break through doors to get to them. So far, I'd replaced two cabinet doors, and had a piece of plywood covering a hole in my pantry door.

After dropping a few treats into his dish, I continued to my bedroom to clean-up. Stepping out of the shower, I could hear my office phone ringing. I toweled off, pulled on a pair of loose-fitting jeans, lightweight V-neck sweater, and boot socks, and then remembered I'd left my boots downstairs. Releasing my curls from the shower cap, I saw that they needed a little refreshing, so I spritz some water on them, did a headshake, and let them land where they wanted.

According to my office clock, it was just after two p.m. The little light blinked on my phone, reminding me to check the message.

"Ms. Jackson, this is CeCe Stiles. I think I need your help. Can you give me a call back?"

I made a note of her number and pocketed it when a file on my desk labeled Freaky Incidents caught my eye. I'd been reviewing it a few days before Mitchel showed up with Murphy. Flipping through the file, I reviewed my latest note about Mitchel. Then, I saw that I'd started a note describing a car parked outside my house around the time the news broke about the now former Senator Richie. Originally, I'd thought they were the guys Katrina sent to protect me from Mitchel, but they weren't, and I had no clue who they were. They came and went like a shadow.

The notification I'd set to remind me of my meet up with Mrs. Summers buzzed, causing my phone to vibrate on the desk, and interrupted my thoughts. I let Godfrey back outside, grabbed my satchel from the hook near the front door, and headed out.

On my way to Summers' house, I called CeCe Stiles. She picked up on the second ring.

"Ms. Jackson? Thanks for calling me back."

"What's up?"

"I think someone is following me."

"Why would anyone be following you?"

"I don't know, but I've seen the same car a few times now. Once when I got off work a few nights ago. Then, I saw it again yesterday while I was returning to work from doing a bank run." She paused, took a breath before continuing. "I know I'm not being paranoid."

"I didn't say you were."

"But I know it sounds like I am."

"Can you describe the car?"

"It's a two-door white car. That's all I know."

"Did you get a look at the person driving it?"

"No."

"Okay, here's what I want you to do. First, don't panic. It could be nothing, but I want you to see if you can get a few more details about the car's make and model. Also try to get a look at the driver. Is it just one person?"

"Yeah, I think so."

"Also write down the time and place you're seeing the vehicle."

"What if they follow me home?"

I didn't want to cause more alarm than was necessary, so I refrained from telling her whoever it was probably already had.

"Just be diligent about locking doors and windows. If you can, walk with a co-worker at work for the time being, or bring your own coffee. When you arrive home, park in a well-lit spot and pay attention to your surroundings."

"I'm scared. Should I call the police?"

"I get that, but there's really nothing else you can do at this point. The police won't get involved at this stage." CeCe remained quiet. "Trust me. Just do what I've suggested. If anything changes, let me know and I'll see what I can do."

"Okay. Thanks, Ms. Jackson."

"MRS. SUMMERS, THANK you for meeting with me, again."

"Of course, of course. Please come in." She stepped aside, allowing me to pass. "I was running behind and only arrived a few minutes ago. Let me just go and get that watch for you."

I waited in the entryway while she disappeared into the hall. The sound of a door opening and then closing signaled her return.

"Here it is." She handed it to me. "Why did you say you needed it?"

"I'm curious if it's connected in some way to the current case I'm working."

"I see. I hope it helps." She looked away and her eyes fell on a picture of Anna. "Do you think my Anna really committed suicide?"

"I don't know."

"But this case that you think might be related involves a suicide?"

"Yes, it does."

"And was that young lady also seeing an older man?"

"Yes, she was."

"The same man who was seeing Anna?"

"I believe so, Mrs. Summers."

"May I ask his name?"

"I can't tell you anything more now, but when I can, I promise I will. Until I have more solid evidence to give to the police, my victim's case will remain closed, and there won't be any reason for the police to take a second look at Anna's suicide."

She shook her head as though dismissing thoughts she'd rather not entertain. Taking a deep breath, she said, "If there's anything else I can do to help, please let me know."

"I'll return the watch as soon as possible. Thank you."

Chapter Twenty-Three

"GOOD MORNING, DEZ." Stepping from the shower, still dripping, I caught the call on the last ring and hit the speaker button. "Have I awakened you?"

"No, Haithem. I've been up for at least a half hour. What's up?"

"The watch arrived yesterday, and we've had a good look at it. Whoever put it together really knew what they were doing. It's very impressive."

I continued drying off, applying a liberal dollop of lotion to both legs and then my arms.

"Have I caught you at a bad time?"

"No, no, it's fine." I continued applying the lotion. "Dammit!" The lotion bottle slipped from my hand and landed in the toilet. Water splashed up and onto the rim of the seat.

"Are you okay, Dez?"

"I'm fine. Impressive, how?" After using the towel to clean up the seat, I tossed it into the hamper, then reached into the bowl to retrieve the bottle of lotion. Thank goodness I'd flushed it before getting into the shower, otherwise I'd have had to use kitchen tongs or something else to get it out. I set it onto the back of the toilet, then washed my hands.

"There's a micro transmitter housed inside the watch. The metal piece also had one, but as you might recall, we weren't sure why at the time we examined it."

"But you think you know now?"

"The two devices communicate with each other and emit a high frequency. It appears that they also could do this independently; however, if they're near each other, the frequency intensifies at a steady rate."

"What would that do?"

"It's similar to the Mosquito, only much more insidious. I believe that whoever developed this technology is not only monitoring it but also able to manipulate the frequencies from a distance. High or low."

"How?"

"We didn't think much about it until we inspected the watch, but both devices also have nano SIM cards. Your person of interest is likely using a phone to receive the data."

"A burner phone."

"Yes, in all likelihood."

"But why use high or low frequency sound at all?"

"Your person is conducting research. This is someone's experiment and as much as I'd like to say it's 'gone wrong,' it hasn't."

"What do you mean?"

"The design is flawless, and it's doing exactly what it's intended to do."

"And that is?"

"The recipients probably complained of headaches, nausea, and tinnitus. Then, irritability. Current research indicates that consistent exposure to high or low frequencies negatively affects employee productivity. It can even be used to ward off impending attacks. For example, a cruise ship captain could dissuade pirates from targeting them."

"So, my guy is weaponizing sound."

"Yes, it appears that way."

"And each of the women he targeted had pre-existing issues with anxiety and depression."

"That tells me that he's researching not only how to create these psychological affects but also how to exacerbate them."

"Son of a bitch!"

"I can return the watch and give you our written report later this morning. I'm heading to The Lab for a meeting with Dawn on another matter."

Tracer operated two investigative labs, one in Lincoln and the other in Omaha. They both rival the work done by other, more well-known facilities. Dawn Ryker was recently promoted to director of the north Omaha location. She'd been instrumental in helping me resolve my sister's cold case.

"The meeting should take about an hour."

"Okay, give me a call when you're ready to meet up."

FOR A TUESDAY MORNING, traffic was light as I drove to meet Clive at the warehouse. He'd already lined up contractors to clean things up. I had to admire his drive and ambition, but then I shouldn't be surprised — he also excelled in his previous occupations.

The warehouse wasn't too far from The Lab, but unlike The Lab, its brick structure remained intact. The warehouse sat on a corner comprising two lots surrounded on one side by an empty lot with overgrown weeds. The back of the building butted up to a recently constructed housing development that already attracted a throng of millennials. The entrance to the building was a set of sturdy, wood double doors that opened into a large, mostly empty, expansive room. I still wasn't sure how I'd use all the space, but Clive had plenty of ideas, so I planned to run with his ideas unless they proved to be awful choices.

"Ms. D!" Clive called out when he saw me. He stood near the only desk in the space at the opposite end of the room. In front of it was an old, smelly couch. It was the kind you never sat on for fear of catching or finding something you didn't want touching your body. A heavy-set, dark-skinned man wearing a construction hat and reviewing a blueprint looked my direction as I approached. "This is Frank Hawthorne," Clive said. "He heads up the crew."

"Nice to meet you," I said, extending my hand.

"Likewise," he greeted me with a voice reminiscent of Barry White and a smile to match.

"When did you get blueprints done?"

"These? Oh, I've had 'em for a while."

Of course, he had.

Looking around for what seemed like the first time, I said, "There's a lot of clean-up before any of this can happen."

"That's why my friend Frank is here. He's got the fastest crew on the north side."

"And what's this going to cost me?"

"My man Frank is reasonable, Ms. D. You don't need to worry about that."

"Our prices are competitive, Ms. Jackson. I've done work for Katrina for a long time," Frank said.

That was all the information I needed. Katrina only liked making money. Parting with it was an entirely different story, so I was probably safe using Frank's company.

"Let me see the plans, then."

Clive began explaining how each level would look. He wanted to convert the three-story building into a multi-use space. The plans included meeting spaces, a spot for a café or small restaurant, a laundry facility in the basement along with a recreation area, and a combination of efficiency and two-bedroom apartments on the top floor.

"Jesus, Clive, there's a lot going on here."

"I told you, I'll manage everything. You don't need to worry about any of it." He pointed to a spot on one of the blueprints. "This is Jackson Investigations." The spot he'd selected was on the ground floor near the back of the building. "There's an exit to the back." His pen identified it for me. "You'll have a private office, reception area, small conference room, and there's space for staff."

"I really don't need all this, Clive."

"Ah, but you will." He said with his finger, emphasizing his point. "You gotta think big, Ms. D."

"That might be too big."

"Nah, just wait and see. You're gonna love it."

"And here's the best part," his finger circled an area on one of the prints. "The basement has a controlled-access workout room for residents. People love that shit. I figured since we don't have a pool, we'd have this."

I hadn't been in the building more than thirty minutes, and I was already drained.

"You need to be more open, Ms. D."

"You two seem to have a few things to discuss. I'll leave you to it." Frank said, picking up a tool belt before walking away.

"Clive, this is too much. I told you I don't want to be a landlord. And you're supposed to be working for me, not managing this."

"I won't be. I've got a management company lined up to take care of all this."

"You've been busy. Am I not giving you enough to do?"

"I'm industrious." Clive had a way of smiling that made me feel like I was getting suckered. "This is a gold mine waiting to be tapped. Why should white people be the only ones to benefit from all this gentrification going on down here?"

He had a valid point. Still, this was my first foray into property investment, and I wasn't convinced it was wise. I had zero patience for other people's bullshit, and like Katrina, getting paid mattered to me.

"I assume you have a budget put together."

He reached into his backpack and pulled out a black, three-ringed binder. Handing it to me, he said, "No doubt. I was very thorough."

Flipping through the first pages, that much was obvious, and I should have expected it considering how he'd handled the tasks I'd assigned him during the previous months.

"How did you get Frank to start on the work without a deposit?"

"We go way back."

"What does that mean exactly?"

Clive's eyes hit the ground, and his feet danced.

"Clive?"

"Okay, okay." His hands raised as if he were giving up. "Katrina arranged it."

"Katrina? Why would she do that?"

"So, what happened was, I, um,"

"Get on with it, Clive."

"I stopped by Easy Street to deliver a message from Detrick and while I was there, Katrina asked about the building. I may have sort of mentioned that you bought it off Detrick."

"Let me guess, she wants the building, and that's how you got these." I pointed to the blueprints.

He shrugged.

"So basically, she's trying to get it designed the way she wants it so when she approaches me with an offer to buy, everything is already in place. Nice, Clive."

"Yeah, but we're not planning to sell. So really, she just helped with the design."

"Blueprints aren't free, and neither is Frank. If she paid for these and him, we already have a problem."

"She was just doing me a favor," he insisted. "She feels bad about Detrick doing time is all."

"That's not how Katrina works, Clive." I checked the time on my phone. "I gotta get going." Pulling my checkbook from my satchel, I ripped out a blank check, then wrote it for an amount I hoped covered the deposit. "Give this to Frank and tell him to give Katrina back her money. And Clive?" I said as I headed for the door. "Stay away from Katrina."

I'd parked along the empty curb across the street from the warehouse, but now there wasn't a single unoccupied space. For a few minutes, I leaned against the Jeep to take in my surroundings. The neighborhood was a mix of residential and small businesses. A steady flow of people entered a bakery, a barbershop, and a small convenience store further down from the warehouse. The aroma of barbecue wafted through the air and my eyes searched for its origins. There was a smokehouse just south of the warehouse. Clive was right about one thing. Gentrification didn't have to only benefit a subset of the population.

As I climbed into my Jeep, I felt the vibration of my phone in my jacket pocket. Pulling it out, I saw Haithem's name.

"Finished?"

"Just now. Where would you like to meet?"

"I'll come to you. I'm not far from The Lab. Maybe five minutes at the most."

"I'll wait in the parking lot," he said, and the call ended.

REPORT IN HAND, I HEADED to meet Detectives Halliday and McDonough at the downtown precinct. They still had the metal card. Now that I had the watch, plus the report from Tracer, I was hoping it would interest them enough to check into my theory about Rick Castle. Detective Halliday led me into the same conference room we sat in days earlier, offered me a seat, and rolled out a chair for himself.

"McDonough will be here shortly. Can I get you a coffee?"

That was new. In all our interactions since I returned to Omaha, never had Detective Halliday offered me anything, except a snide remark or chastisement for getting in his way. To say he wasn't a fan of private investigators was an understatement. Maybe Dick Swan sullied our reputation with him. I'd heard they were partners when they started with the force.

"I'm good, thanks." I slid the report across the table with the watch on top like it was a gift. "Here's what I've got."

McDonough entered the room, coffee cup in one hand, and a file in the other. He took the seat next to his partner.

"Good morning again, Ms. Jackson. What have you got for us today?"

I removed a set of pictures from a file in my satchel and added them to the selection in front of Detective Halliday.

"What am I looking at?"

"That device is a nano transmitter that came from inside that watch. There's also one inside the metal card I gave you. Tracer's report establishes that the two devices are, in fact, communicating with each other."

McDonough reached for the watch to scrutinize it while Detective Halliday thumbed through the two-page report.

"It says here that they're likely using high and low frequencies with the goal of affecting the end user's physiological and psychological states."

"Exactly. Rick Castle developed the watches, and I believe he placed the metal card on the backside of a wall-mounted clock in Libby Walker's apartment. Wait, I have another," I searched through my Walker file and found the image of the wall in her apartment. "Something is missing here." I pointed to the image. "That's about the right amount of room for a clock."

"Where's the clock?"

"I don't know. Susie Walker says it was gone when she came to the apartment the first time after she found her sister. Apparently, it was a decorative clock and a gift from,"

"Our new friend Mr. Castle," Detective McDonough said.

I nodded. "I don't think he gave clocks to CeCe Stiles or Anna Summers. At least, CeCe didn't mention it when I spoke with her. Castle did take the watch back from her, but he couldn't get this one from Anna. I'm betting, though, that he has Libby's. I also think he has the clock."

"And you believe, what? Somehow this guy used sound to harm these women?" McDonough asked.

"There's enough research now to support using high and low frequencies to cause irritability, anxiety, and depression. Each one of these women had bouts of anxiety or mild-to-moderate depression. Libby Walker,"

"Was taking anti-depressants," Halliday said.

"What if his little experiment pushed Libby and Anna over the edge? Tracer's report also shows that whoever created the devices could easily monitor and control them remotely using a smartphone."

"All right, Jackson. You've convinced me." Halliday stacked the images atop the report and placed the watch on top.

"So, you'll take another look?"

"Yeah, we'll take another look, but you need to back off, now."

I put my hands up in front of me. "Not a problem. All I want is to tell Susie Walker what really happened to her sister and give some peace of mind to Anna Summers' mother."

Detectives Halliday and McDonough rolled their chairs back, queuing me to do the same. I stood, shook both their hands, and thanked them for their time.

I HAD TO ADMIT I FELT good after my meeting with the detectives. I'd figured out the connection between Castle and the women, with a little help from Tracer, and I could tell Susie she was right about him. To top it all off, Mrs. Summers also would know that her daughter didn't commit suicide of her own volition.

Eventually the detectives would get what they needed for the DA to charge Rick Castle in the death of both women and Libby Walker's unborn child. Still, he had money so there was no guarantee it all would go the way it should, but things looked promising.

Walking into Hy-Vee, I saw Susie checking out a customer. She saw me, smiled, and then finished her task.

"Can we talk a minute?"

"Yeah, just give me a sec." She placed a closed sign at the end of her lane and turned her register light on to get her manager's attention. A tall, thin man named Mike walked over to check on Susie.

"What's up?" He asked.

"Can I step away for a few minutes? This is Dezeray Jackson, the PI I told you about."

"Sure, take your time. I'll handle things here for a few minutes."

I followed Susie to a staff break room lined with lockers. The rest of the space contained three white round tables with matching chairs, a refrigerator, and a long counter with two microwaves, a sink, and cabinets below. Two other employees chatted at one table, so we sat at an unoccupied one a little further away from them.

"What's happened?" Susie asked.

"I just met with the detectives involved in your sister's original case. They've agreed to take a second look."

She sighed like a weight vest had been removed from her shoulders.

"Really?"

"Yes."

"And I was right about Rick Castle?"

"It looks like it."

I explained everything I knew up to that point and what I'd given to the detectives. Susie's face paled when I told her about Castle's apparent experiment. When I finished, she took a deep breath, her shoulders raised to the bottom of her earlobes, then settled again as she closed her eyes.

Opening her eyes she said, "So, now we wait."

"Pretty much, but at least now you know."

"Yeah, now I know."

MY NEXT STOP WAS TO see Mrs. Summers. When I called, she was just leaving work, and we agreed to meet up at her house at six-fifteen. I arrived before her and parked on the street in front of her place. At six-twenty, her silver Prius pulled into the driveway. I gave her a minute to get out of her car and then stepped out to meet her.

"Ms. Jackson,"

"Dez. You can call me Dez."

She strung a purse over one shoulder, and reached back inside to grab another bag, then closed the car door.

"Shall we go inside, or,"

"This will only take a second. I mean unless you'd rather go inside?"

"No, this is fine."

"The police are re-opening the case I've been investigating."

"The one you believe might be related to my daughter's death?"

"Yes. I don't think your daughter committed suicide of her own free will. I think she was pushed to do it."

"How is that even possible?"

I recapped what I'd uncovered and provided to the detectives. "So, chances are you'll receive a visit from them. I'm sorry about the watch."

"If it helps prove that Anna and that other young lady, what did you say her name was?"

"Libby. Libby Walker."

"If it helps prove they didn't commit suicide, then I don't need the watch. And to be honest, I wouldn't want anything that Rick Castle used to cause my Anna harm. I hope he rots in prison."

"You and me both, believe me."

I said goodbye to Mrs. Summers and was still feeling accomplished as I drove to Eddy's. It's rare that I get to deliver good news to someone who isn't a client and today was a two-for-one special.

WHEN I ARRIVED AT EDDY'S the only available parking was two blocks away, which on a Tuesday night seemed odd, especially at seven o'clock. As I got closer, I could see a line of people outside the door that continued around the corner. Mack was checking IDs when I walked up to him.

"Hey, Ms. D."

"What's going on?"

"Tournament. Starts at eight."

"When did that become a thing?"

"It's just something Big E's trying." He checked a few more IDs, allowing several people to enter. "You can go on in if you want."

I slid past him, and in front of a few players hiding their cues in cases. It'd been years since I watched any tournament action, and since I had nowhere else to be, I figured I'd order my usual and partake in the free entertainment. Eddy stood behind the bar, arms folded across his chest as his bartenders filled orders. At the far end, an empty stool called my name. Eddy walked over when he saw me.

"Busy night," I said, taking the seat.

"Yeah, I'm trying something new. Tuesdays have been getting too slow." He filled a glass with water, tossed in a sliced lemon, and set it in front of me on a coaster.

"Usual?" He asked.

"You know it."

He turned to the kitchen and shouted my order to Dwayne. "Beer or gin & tonic?"

"Beer, thanks." Eddy turned to one of the bartenders and told them to get my beer. "What's the entry fee?"

"Why, you want to play?"

"Nah, just curious."

"$100 per person."

"That's reasonable."

"Good size crowd, too. You know, I used to run these tournaments all the time back when your pops was around. You remember that?"

I shook my head.

"It was good money. Not as good as playing, but still decent enough. How is your dad? I haven't talked to him in a while."

"He's good. Seems to like Baltimore."

I noticed Eddy looking past me and turned to see where his gaze had fallen, and my knees smacked into Murphy.

"What are you doing here?" I asked. He leaned in and kissed my forehead.

"Hello to you to sunshine."

He removed his leather jacket and set it on the back of an empty seat next to me, then sat down. The two bulls exchanged wordless nods, then Eddy produced another beer and set it in front of Murphy.

"How'd you know I was here?" I asked.

Murphy grinned and shook his head.

"I thought you left town."

"I thought you might want to hear the news from me."

"What news?"

"Mitchel's dead. Someone got to him in his cell."

I had just taken a drink and nearly sprayed Eddy with my beer.

"What the hell happened?"

"My guess? The Senator happened. You know he couldn't afford for anyone to know everything Mitchel had his hands in."

I stared back at Murphy trying to comprehend what he'd just explained. He had every intention of taking Mitchel out as soon as an opportunity presented itself.

"What? You think I had something to do with Mitchel's death?"

"It had crossed my mind."

"I told you someone was going to take care of him one way or another. I didn't say it would necessarily be me, as much as I would have enjoyed that." He sipped his beer and stole a few fries from the plate Eddy had just delivered. I slapped his hand.

"What? You can share. French fries are bad for you."

"I gotta say, I'm relieved."

"I figured you would be. That shit got what he deserved."

"You want something to eat?"

"Nah, I'll just keep stealing from your plate." His hand caressed my leg, and he leaned in and stole another fry with his left.

Eddy had walked away to deal with the tournament action, but one of the bartenders saw my signal.

"Can you get another cheeseburger and fries for this one here, so he'll stop," I caught Murphy's wrist mid-grab, "Stealing mine?"

"Sure thing, Ms. D."

"You come here too much. It's like Cheers." Murphy scooted his chair closer. "How about we get that to go?"

"What? And miss all this?" I gestured to the now wall-to-wall throng of players and spectators that had filled the pool hall. Murphy leaned in; I could feel the heat of his breath on my neck as his lips grazed my ear.

"Can we get that order to go, please?" I said.

Chapter Twenty-Four

"YOU SHOULD PROBABLY let him out." Murphy rolled over and pulled me to him. I could hear Godfrey whining outside the bedroom door.

"He can wait a little longer." I pulled the blanket snug beneath my chin and nestled deeper into Murphy's chest. "It's too early to get up."

"It's eight-thirty, love."

I sat straight up. "Shit!"

"That's what I was afraid he might do." Murphy sat up; his head supported by his fist. A slow smirk spread across his face. I punched his chest, and he trapped my hand to him, pulling me closer. He teased my lips with his tongue before kissing me. "I missed you, love."

"Yeah, yeah. I've got to get up." I pushed off him, grabbed my silk robe, and retreated to the bathroom. When I returned, Murphy had dealt with Godfrey, so I took a quick shower before heading downstairs.

The aroma of fresh-brewed coffee, bacon, eggs, and toast greeted me as I entered the kitchen. Murphy buttered toast and added strawberry jam to each slice before bringing them to the table where he had already set out a mug of Breakfast Serenade for me. The chair legs scraped across the linoleum when I pulled it back.

"What's the occasion?" I asked, reaching for my tea.

"What? Can't a guy do something special for his,"

"His what, exactly."

Murphy smiled his crooked smile, kissed my forehead, and sat across from me.

"It's getting cold. I know how much you hate it when your food gets cold." He took a bite of his bacon and followed it with eggs, then the coffee.

"I know better than to get used to this." I used my fork to gesture at the now crowded table. "This, my friend, is not your style."

"But what if it is?"

"It isn't."

"But what if I wanted it to be?"

"Murphy get a grip. You're not a homebody. You can't even stay put for more than a week, two tops, before you get that itch. Stop trying to be something you're not."

"Fair enough. Don't say I didn't put forth a valiant effort, though."

"I don't expect anything from this, whatever you want to call it, other than a good lay, great take out, and an occasional movie moment." I said, shoving a forkful of eggs into my mouth.

"Good, I'm glad to know we're still on the same page."

"We are. Don't worry about that."

"Nice chat," I said, standing up to clear my dishes. "Lock up on your way out."

Murphy reached for my free wrist, and I turned back.

"You mean more to me than that."

"I know."

IT'D BEEN WEEKS SINCE I got in touch with my friend Cynthia Cruz. With everything that had been going on with the Kincade case and then Libby Walker, the days just slipped past. So, when she called suggesting we get lunch, I was happy to oblige. We decided to meet at Brazen Head, which I knew meant we'd be there for a while. It's hard to resist a good beer, great pub food, free music, and the eye candy that was her boyfriend, Mick.

His broad smile greeted us from behind the hand carved, smooth-to-the-touch walnut stained wood bar. We sauntered up and pulled out two chairs. Mick leaned forward to give Cynthia a quick kiss. Her caramel-colored skin took on a red hue that faded moments later.

"Looking lovely as usual, ladies."

Irish male accents have a way of relieving a woman of her intimate apparel. It certainly was one of the things that made Murphy so damned irresistible. He could turn it on and off like a faucet whenever he liked. Mick, having not been born in the US, was one hundred percent Irish twenty-four-seven, and I knew that had to be tough for Cynthia to resist. She'd always been attracted to the strong, understated type who could kick ass without much effort, but would rather resolve disputes peacefully.

"What can I get you this afternoon?"

We both ordered Chardonnay and nachos to share. After Mick returned with our wine, we moved to a corner table to catch up.

"So, what you're telling me is that you just identified a serial killer."

I nearly spat out a mouthful of wine.

"Uh, no. I wouldn't classify him as a serial killer."

"The suspect has a specific type of young woman that he targets. You know about three women he's had relationships with, two of whom are, in fact, dead. He gives them gifts that manipulate them physically and mentally." Chip in hand, Cynthia continued, "I don't know, in my book that makes him, at the very least, a serial killer wanna-be." She crunched down on the chip, then washed it down with a few sips of her wine. "Dez, I think you might have just saved a lot of other women from this guy."

"I can't believe you hadn't heard anything about it."

"I wasn't hanging out at that precinct the past few days."

Cynthia worked for The Herald as an investigative journalist and proved to be a tremendous help during more than one of my cases. She would have made a great PI except for her aversion to weapons and staying up late.

"Now you can run with it. I'm sure the detectives will be eager to talk with you."

"They always are," she said, stifling a laugh. "But seriously, can you imagine what it must be like to be his wife? I mean, she had to know something was going on."

"Not necessarily."

"But she did hire a PI, so she obviously thought he was up to something. I bet he's done it before."

"Wait, what do you mean, 'before?'"

"What are the odds that a creep like Castle just started these little experiments when they came to Nebraska?" She finished her wine and signaled to Mick for another round. "I'm telling you, he's done something like this before, and I'd bet a Benjamin this isn't the first time she's hired a PI to check on her husband."

I hadn't even considered that angle until now. There probably were others that we'd never know about unless either Castle confessed, or his wife acknowledged the previous affairs he'd had. Castle didn't strike me as the kind of guy who'd confess to anything except his own intelligence. His wife, on the other hand, seemed ready to come unhinged. It wouldn't hurt to follow that trail a bit farther to see where it might lead.

"As always, Cyn, you've opened my eyes to another perspective." I raised my glass to her.

"Anything I can do to help the cause."

Chapter Twenty-Five

PATRICIA CASTLE AGREED to meet with me Friday afternoon at a diner off I-80 west. She chose a location on the outskirts of Omaha that was miles away from where they lived. Maybe she was one of those people who liked that show Diners, Drive-Ins, and Dives, but she didn't strike me as that type. I was that type one hundred percent. The place she chose is one of my favorites.

Stepping inside Big Moe's was like falling backward off a high dive. At first you think, "I must be crazy to do this," but then a surge of adrenaline kicks in and you take the plunge. The place had a less than stellar reputation for its food, with an average rating of two and half stars, but since I'd never gotten sick, I kept coming back. It was like roulette, but they had the best griddle cakes in a hundred-mile radius. I'd bet money on that any day of the week.

I spotted Patricia at a booth with a view of the gas pumps. She wore her hair in a messy bun atop her head, and her face seemed paler than on previous occasions when we'd met.

"Thanks for meeting me, Patricia." I said, sliding into the seat across from hers.

"You gave me the impression that whatever you needed was urgent."

I found her statement interesting considering she took her time returning my call, but I let it go.

A server approached our table, pad flipped open, and pen in hand.

"What can a get ya?"

Patricia ordered a Sprite and a basket of fries with a side of Blue Cheese dressing. It was a strange combination and reinforced the fact that the Castle's weren't from Nebraska. Everyone knows the only condiment you put with fries is ketchup. I ordered a Coke knowing that the caffeine this late in the afternoon would screw with my sleep, but it was a Friday, so I'd likely be up late, anyway. The woman hurried away, and I returned my focus to Patricia.

"I need to ask you something and I know it might make you uncomfortable."

"It's about Rick."

"Yes. Was this the first time you hired a private investigator to spy on your husband?"

Patricia Castle looked straight into my eyes and lied. I knew this like I knew a winter storm on the second day of spring in Nebraska was a high probability. She maintained eye contact longer than was normal. It wasn't just that, though. I'd caught an upward tug of the corner of her mouth just before she answered.

"It's just that it seems likely that your husband didn't just start having affairs when you arrived in Omaha."

"We were happy once. Coming to Omaha changed things." Her gaze focused to something outside. "It changed him."

"How so?"

"Rick has always been ambitious and driven. It's one reason I married him, but this job." She shrugged; her head moved side to side as though she didn't believe what she was saying. "It brought out the worst in him."

"So, you think the affairs had to do with his job?"

"I think it was his way of coping with the stress."

"Still, I can't imagine that his work in former positions was any less stressful. What made this unique?"

Patricia shifted in her seat and reached for the saltshaker, placing it midway between us on the table. The server arrived with her order and set it onto the table so we both could reach the basket.

"Would you like some? I can't possibly eat all these."

"No, thanks. Patricia, two of the three women your husband had affairs with are dead."

"I realize that."

She was as wound up as a new ball of yarn. Getting her to admit she'd hired an investigator prior to Anderson wouldn't be easy.

"When did you suspect that he was unfaithful?"

"I don't remember now." She reached for a French Fry and dipped it into the dressing. "I suppose it was more than a year ago."

"Why'd you wait so long to hire Matt Anderson?"

"You've never been married, have you?"

I shook my head. Marriage interested me about as much as having children. Both meant a complete loss of freedom.

"I didn't want to believe it."

"What changed?"

She shrugged, again. "Our kids are getting older and soon they'll be off on their own."

Patricia Castle was afraid of being alone. That's what this was all about. She hired Anderson to confirm what she suspected, and when he told her the truth, she snapped. But not because the affairs were something new.

"When did you confront Rick?"

"Excuse me?"

"When did you tell Rick that you knew about the other women?"

"I didn't. He still doesn't know that I know."

"Why keep it from him?"

"Those relationships are over. It serves no purpose to,"

"Libby Walker is dead because of your husband."

"You don't know that. You can't possibly know that." Her voice had risen at least an octave, but then she smoothed her napkin on the table, folded it, and set it to the side. "My husband is a lot of things, but he's not a killer, and I won't have you or anyone else,"

I raised my hands in front of me to signal I was giving up, "Look, he's connected. That much I know. How or why is up to the police to figure out. But don't you think Libby Walker's mother deserves to know the truth about her daughter's death? Surely, you can empathize."

She inhaled and exhaled slowly. "Of course, I can, but Rick isn't guilty of anything except poor judgment."

"And getting Libby Walker pregnant."

"You know as well as I do that a woman who chooses not to protect herself wants to get pregnant. She was trying to trap my husband — force him to leave me. Obviously, when he didn't fall for that, she killed herself. He can't be blamed for that."

"Just to be clear, you never hired anyone to investigate your husband before hiring Matt Anderson. Is that correct?"

"Yes, that is correct."

After saying goodbye, I returned to my Jeep with the all-to-familiar feeling I'd honed after years of investigative training. My gut told me Patricia Castle was lying, but I didn't know who she was trying to protect — her husband or someone else.

I'D GOTTEN TO BED LATE, so when I heard the nails on the chalkboard ring from my phone, my hand instinctively groped for it next to my bed. I missed, sending it tumbling to the floor. The incessant ring continued. Leaning over the edge of my bed, eyes still partially closed, I snatched it up.

"Ms. Jackson?"

"Who is this?"

"CeCe Stiles. I got a picture of that license plate. I mean, I think I got some of it, anyway."

"Send it to me. I'll see what I can find out."

I disconnected, stretched, and checked the time. At least she'd had the decency to wait until after eight o'clock on a Saturday morning to call me. Knowing there wasn't much I could do with a partial plate for a case that lacked urgency to the police, I opted not to bother calling the detectives with my newly acquired information. Instead, I'd toss it to Clive to test his resource capabilities.

After a quick clean-up, I grabbed a leash and took Godfrey for a walk around the block. Dr. Roberts wanted me to keep Godfrey moving, but to ease him into it. His recovery had been steady, and he was moving around better every day. Whenever I looked at him, my mind returned to Mitchel's face. I couldn't help but be thankful that someone took care of him, so Murphy didn't have to.

As Godfrey pulled on the leash, urging me to move faster, I reminded him with a gentle tug to slow down. He accommodated my request with an abrupt stop that nearly had me tripping over him.

"Godfrey!"

His big brown eyes looked up at me and I swear he was grinning.

"That's not funny, Godfrey. Let's go."

Our walk took less than thirty minutes, and by the time we rounded the corner up the block from the house, Godfrey was panting. Dropping his leash at the foot of the front door, I could hear my office phone ringing as I unlocked it. Godfrey pushed the door inward and before I could unhook his leash, he trotted to the kitchen. The phone stopped ringing just as I retrieved it from its charging station, but then my back pocket vibrated.

"Ms. D, good morning. Oh wait, it's almost afternoon. Anyway, I got your message about that plate, and I tracked it down."

Even I had to marvel at his speed.

"That might be a record for you, Clive."

"Huh. Yeah, maybe." He laughed. "The plate is registered to Evan Castle."

"That's Castle's son?"

"Yep."

"What would he be doing following CeCe Stiles around? And how would he know who she is?"

"Maybe he doesn't. Maybe it's just a coincidence."

"I don't believe in coincidences." I sounded like Murphy.

"What are you gonna do?"

"I guess I'm following a teenage high school student around for a while."

MONDAY MORNING, I WOKE at the crack of dawn to hightail it over to the Castle's place. I wanted to make sure I knew every place Evan castle traveled. He was a senior, which came with a few privileges at most high schools.

I parked my Jeep several houses from theirs and waited. At shortly before seven-thirty, a two-door white Nissan Altima backed out of the garage and rolled to the end of the driveway. From my vantage point, I could see a girl in the passenger seat and assumed that she was Emily Castle. Evan sped through the streets of his neighborhood, arriving at Marian High School ten minutes later. Emily stepped from the car, shoved the door shut with her hip, and walked to the entrance, greeting a few girls along the way.

Creighton Prep is about fifteen minutes from Marian, but Evan cut that time down by several minutes, easing the Altima into a parking spot at the rear of the school. Figuring Prep probably didn't police their parking lot, I found a spot in view of his car and the door he'd entered. Then I waited.

By eleven o'clock, my stomach started rumbling, I rummaged through my cooler knowing it didn't have what I wanted — a raspberry filled donut. I downed a juice box hoping that would satisfy my sugar craving and followed that with a Colby Jack cheese stick and a package of mixed nuts. Around lunch time, Evan Castle exited the building, hopped into his car, and left the lot, with me close behind.

He stopped at a vape place first, returning to his car empty-handed, then went through a Burger King drive-thru before heading back to school. I spent the remainder of the afternoon sitting in my Jeep doing word search puzzles via an app and watching the door. At dismissal, I followed him back to Marian to retrieve his sister. From there, the two drove home. At five-thirty, Patricia Castle arrived home, by which time my ass was numb. I got out of my Jeep, went around the back to the opposite sidewalk, stretched, and then returned to the front. The low rumble and screech of a garage door opening and closing caught my attention.

The Altima rolled down the driveway and headed the opposite direction. Hopping into my car, I fumbled with my keys, dropped them on the floor, and bumped my head trying to pick them up. The engine of the Altima faded in the distance. Finally getting the Jeep started, I shifted into drive and had to make up a few blocks to catch up with Evan.

The car swerved in and out of traffic along Dodge Street and headed east toward downtown while most everyone else drove west, escaping their nine-to-five. Aside from a job at a grocery store near their home, Evan spent much of his time involved in school activities, none of which involved a trip to downtown Omaha on a Monday night.

The Altima turned left at Saddle Creek Road and traveled north to Cuming Street, heading east and eventually turning left at Burt Street. Evan continued past the North Freeway. When he reached 10th Street and headed south, I had a hunch where he might be going. The bistro wasn't far from where he'd parked. I tucked my Jeep a few spaces back from his car and waited for him to get out.

Patricia Castle stepped from the Altima wearing a baseball cap with her hair tucked beneath it. Large, black sunglasses obscured her face, and she pulled her jacket collar up to cover her neck. When she started walking toward Howard Street, I got out of my Jeep and followed her.

As she approached the building, she stopped short, deciding to sit on a bench outside. The sun had disappeared as dusk settled in and the temperature dropped. From across the street, I concealed myself near the corner of a candy shop. Patricia tapped at her phone, then shoved it into a chest pocket. Clouds formed in the sky threatening to unleash cats, dogs, and probably a few gerbils. Whatever she was doing here, I hoped would happen before that.

At six forty-five, CeCe Stiles exited the bistro, turned right, and walked past Castle. She let CeCe get several feet ahead before stalking her. I jogged across the street, following both women from a few yards back. When CeCe halted, turned, and confronted Patricia, I dropped to one knee pretending to remove something from my shoe, and waited.

"Why are you following me?"

Patricia Castle hadn't expected this. To be honest, neither did I. CeCe had struck me as mousy.

CeCe asked again, this time the pitch of her voice much higher than before.

"I — I want to ask you about someone I think we both know," Patricia countered.

"Who?" CeCe stood, hands on her hips and head tilted.

"Rick Castle."

"You're his wife." CeCe started backing away as Patricia moved closer. "I don't know what you want, but I haven't had anything to do with your husband in a long time."

"But you were seeing him, weren't you?" Her tone was calm, almost reassuring.

"Look, I don't have anything to say to you about him." She backed closer into a railing outside The Passageway.

Patricia stepped forward, again.

"You should talk to your husband, not me. I ended it, not him."
CeCe turned and disappeared into the building.

I crossed the street and headed back toward 10th Street,
keeping in step with Patricia as she made her way back to her car.
Large raindrops smacked the ground, promising the onslaught of a
cascade.

THE OMAHA COMMUNITY is reeling from the arrest of
world-renowned researcher Rick Castle. It happened just moments
ago. Our sources say that Dr. Castle is being held in connection
with the death of Libby Walker, a former UNO student.

"Turn that up," I shouted at Clive over the banging of
hammers. He'd called this morning and asked me to come to the
warehouse to review a few minor changes to the renovation plans.
Telling him I didn't care what changed didn't work. After a shower,
light breakfast, and my third cup of Tea Trove Black, I was ready to
deal with the project. Luckily, I'd missed morning traffic heading
east.

When I arrived, Clive sat at his old desk with the blueprints
spread across it and wearing a hard hat. A nearby retro style
boombox tuned to a local station sat on a workbench with a small
TV next to it. Clive reached for the remote and increased the
volume for the TV.

Rick Castle is a researcher for SMT Tech, where his focus has been on the weaponization of sound waves. Sources close to the investigation say that he had an intimate relationship with Ms. Walker. She died of an apparent suicide. My sources also say that Ms. Walker was pregnant at the time of her death. The Walker family could not be reached for comment. This is a developing story, and we will keep you informed as we learn more.

"I've got to go," I said, tossing my satchel over my shoulder.

"But what about the plans?"

"Looks good to me! You're a natural at this whole project management stuff." As the door shut behind me, I added, "I'll be in touch later."

Chapter Twenty-Six

SUSIE WALKER WAS IN her usual spot at a register near the self-checkout lanes when I entered Hy-Vee. Most of the customers were in the seventy plus group, picking up a few odds and ends. Others were there for the buffet and to get the latest gossip.

After Susie helped her last customer, I approached the register grabbing a Coke and a pack of gum from the displays.

"Dez! What are you doing here?"

"Have you heard the news, yet?"

She shook her head.

"Not since before I left this morning. Why? What's up?"

"The police have arrested Rick Castle."

Her hand instinctively rose to cover her mouth.

"I don't have any more details. The report was incomplete, but it looks like the detectives took what I offered them to heart and did a little more digging."

"Oh, my god. I can't believe it."

"It's just a matter of time before they connect everything to him."

"Yeah, and his wife. They both deserve to go to prison for the rest of their lives."

"Wait, what are you talking about?"

"I didn't tell you?"

I looked at her blankly and waited.

"I found Libby's diary."

"And?"

"Excuse me, but is this lane still open?" An elderly woman wearing sweatpants, a T-shirt, and a baseball cap stood behind a cart filled with fruits, vegetables, and a few bottles of wine.

"Yes, ma'am." Susie said as she finished ringing up my items. "Give me a sec."

Grabbing my items, I headed to the café. A few minutes later, Susie joined me at a table.

"Libby talked about meeting some woman. I can only assume it was Castle's wife. I mean, who else could it be?"

"Just about anyone."

"No, no. The dates match with when she was seeing him."

"What'd Libby write?"

"She was scared because she thought someone was following her. There were a few pages about that. It seemed like it happened a handful of times."

"Did she describe the woman?"

"No, but then in a later entry she wrote that the woman found her on campus and told her to get rid of the baby."

"Where's the diary now?"

"My apartment."

"I think we're going to need to give it to the police, Susie."

She nodded and smiled. "Yeah, that's what I was just thinking."

AS ENLIGHTENING AS my sit down with Susie was, I wasn't convinced Patricia Castle had anything to do with Libby Walker's death. Sure, I could see her approaching the girl, but I just couldn't see how Patricia could have killed her. Still, I needed to have a conversation with her to be certain.

News crews camped outside the Castle residence made navigating the street difficult. I ended up parking two blocks away and heel-toe expressing it back to their house. The blinds and curtains were drawn in every front-facing window. From the sidewalk I could see a sign on the door that read, "Please respect our privacy" in black Sharpie. Making my way to the door, a reporter stopped me.

"Are you the Castle's attorney?"

"No, just a family friend."

"Would you like to comment on Rick Castle's arrest?"

"No, I wouldn't," I said pushing past him.

I knocked, but when no one answered, I pulled out my phone and called Patricia's cell.

"This is Dez Jackson. I'm outside."

Several minutes later, the door opened. The crews were all abuzz, and cameras flashed, but there wasn't anyone to see except me. I stepped inside, and the door closed behind me.

"Can you believe this?" Patricia Castle paced in the entryway. Her son and daughter sat, each on a stair, leading to the second level of their home.

"Perhaps it would be best if they found something to distract themselves." I gestured to Evan and Emily.

"What could they possibly do that would accomplish that? Have you looked outside?" Her trill voice cut through the air.

"I suppose not."

She stopped pacing and then stared at me; a confused expression settled on her face.

"What are you doing here?"

"I need to ask you some questions about Libby Walker."

"Now? You need to ask me now?"

"Yeah, I kinda do, but I'd rather not in front of your kids."

She looked from me to them and back again before ordering them to go to their rooms. Two doors slammed, one followed by another. Soon after, drum and bass beats drowned out the commotion I'd stirred upon entering the house.

"What the hell is this all about?" Patricia asked as she led me into the living room.

"Libby Walker kept a diary."

"So? What has that got to do with me?"

"In it she described a few instances of being followed, and a conversation with you. You told me you didn't know Libby Walker. You'd never met her."

"Look, I think you can plainly see that I have bigger concerns at the moment." She made sweeping gestures toward the front of the house.

"You told her to have an abortion."

Patricia stood near a large, white sofa. The space was one of those rooms that looked like no one ever used it. Everything from the perfectly placed pillows to the art arrangements, and nothing personal like shoes, or backpacks told me this was their showroom.

"Okay, yes, I met the girl. What do you want me to say? I couldn't have her ripping my family apart."

"What happened?"

"What do you mean, 'what happened'? We spoke. The stupid girl insisted that she wanted to keep it. Can you imagine? She has no money, so obviously she planned to blackmail Rick." Patricia reminded me of a tiger trapped in a zoo cage as she moved from the fireplace to the couch.

"What did you tell her?"

"I explained to her that the only thing she'd ever receive was money for the child. We would never acknowledge it as a member of our family. Rick would never see it, let alone be part of its life in any meaningful way. He had no intention of giving up our life for a life with her."

"Rick told you about the affair?"

"Yes."

"When did he tell you?"

"What?" The news crews outside distracted her.

"When did Rick tell you about Libby?"

"What difference does that make?"

Her cell phone chirped. She snatched it from the coffee table in front of the couch.

"Yes? Yes, that would be helpful. Thank you. Twenty minutes? Okay." She disconnected and replaced it onto the table. Returning her attention to me, she said, "If you're finished interrogating me, our attorney will be here shortly, and I have more important things to deal with."

With that dismissal, I headed for the door and let myself out. I'd gotten what I came for, so it didn't matter.

Chapter Twenty-Seven

DETECTIVE HALLIDAY and his partner, Detective McDonough sat across from me in the small, now familiar, conference room. I was beginning to feel like I should have a desk in the precinct. Pen in hand, Detective McDonough waited for me to begin.

"You have more information you'd like to share, so what is it?" Halliday asked.

"Patricia Castle knew about Libby Walker and the baby."

"Go on."

Reaching into my leather bag, I removed Libby's diary and slid it across the table.

"What's this?" Halliday asked.

"Libby Walker's diary."

"Where did you get it?"

"Her sister gave it to me."

"How do we know this belonged to Libby Walker and not her sister? Her very distraught sister." McDonough chimed into the conversation, setting his pen down to flip through the diary.

"Get it analyzed. I'm sure there's money in your budget for an expert."

They exchanged glances.

"What's your theory here, Jackson? First you try to convince us the husband did the girl. Now, what? You think it was the wife?"

"I don't know. Maybe." I explained how Patricia followed CeCe Stiles, and that Libby Walker wrote about a woman following her, too.

"Just because Patricia Castle might have followed Libby Walker doesn't mean she had anything to do with her death."

"But what's more plausible, that Rick Castle killed her with sound waves or Patricia Castle did it with pills?"

"What are you saying?"

"Maybe Libby took too many pills or maybe someone helped her take too many pills."

"We haven't placed anyone else in the apartment except you and her sister."

"You've been back to the apartment."

Halliday shook his head.

"Then she wore gloves."

"Look, we appreciate you bringing this in, but we've got this from here on out. I'm sure you've got plenty of other people who need someone with your skill set." Halliday said as he stood to escort me out.

Feeling rebuffed and annoyed, I was starting to think that Libby's death wasn't Rick Castle's doing — at least not entirely. But I needed proof, which I was sorely lacking at the moment. If Patricia Castle met with Libby once, what would have stopped her from meeting with her again? But nothing in the diary indicated that Libby and Patricia met more than once. That didn't mean it didn't happen, though. I was missing something. That annoyed me even more than Halliday and McDonough.

"WHY ARE YOU SET ON the wife?" Eddy asked as he wiped down the counter before placing a beer in front of me. "It's possible she did all you say and didn't kill the girl. 'Sides, you got the husband."

"Maybe, but something feels off."

"When did this Castle woman meet up with your victim?"

"I'm not exactly sure."

"Was it just the one time? You said she followed Walker, and at some point, she confronted her. Where'd that meeting happen?"

"According to the diary, it was on campus, but I don't know where."

"The question you have to ask is would an uppity, well-off, white woman confront her husband's side chick publicly? In my experience, I'd be inclined to believe that wouldn't happen." Eddy tossed the used towel into a bucket with a few others, then hoisted the bucket, placing it out of sight behind the bar.

"Yeah, but the diary states Libby first met Patricia at UNO."

"You already know she followed the girl, so she knew something about her schedule or habits."

"Just like with CeCe Stiles."

"She probably knew where the girl lived, too."

"Maybe she met her twice. There weren't any entries after the one at UNO."

Eddy nodded his head saying, "That's the only thing that makes sense if," the phone behind the bar rang, distracting Eddy mid-sentence. He motioned for one of the doormen to answer it. "If your girl wasn't satisfied with the first encounter."

Following Eddy's line of reasoning, I interjected, "She met her again at the apartment. She had to have, but why would Libby let her inside?"

Chapter Twenty-Eight

AFTER A FITFUL NIGHT'S sleep, I gave up and got out of bed at five-thirty. Godfrey was doing his best impersonation of Balto as I stepped over him to go downstairs. When I lived in New York City, the statue of that husky was the closest I ever thought I'd get to owning a pet.

As I made tea and waited for my bagel to pop from the toaster, the feeling I was missing something in the Castle case dogged me. I couldn't believe Patricia Castle would simply allow Libby Walker to exist. There had to be more to their meeting than what Patricia conveyed. But, what?

With my evenly burnt Everything bagel ready, I smothered it with cream cheese, placed it onto a plate, and grabbed my tea. There wasn't anything for me to do except catch up on the news, so I headed to my office. The computer came to life with a tap on the screen and I settled into my chair.

I read through the Associated Press, then checked out local news sources. Sometimes they provided potential client leads. Pulling out a drawer and rummaging through it, my fingers located a small notepad. A bottle of ibuprofen had rolled to the front. I stared at it for a minute, and then I remembered. There was a prescription bottle with Patricia Castle's name on it on the entryway table in her house. I'd noticed it when I stopped by Thursday. The prescription was for something that started with a 'T'. Googling drugs starting with that letter returned about four hundred results. It was going to be a long morning.

By late afternoon, I'd narrowed my list of drugs down to a handful I thought might negatively interact with Libby Walker's medication. Whichever one it was couldn't raise any alarms for Libby, otherwise she would have probably tried to get help. According to Susie Walker, Libby was taking Zoloft and had been for maybe two months.

Checking the time, I knew exactly who I could hit up for some answers. I put Godfrey outside with food and water just in case I got home later than expected. No Saturday traffic meant going east to The Lab wouldn't be a problem. Parking across the street, I saw Dawn Ryker waiting outside. She smiled as I approached.

"What's up, Dez?"

"Thanks for meeting me on such short notice."

"No problem at all. You gave me an excuse to take a break. Let's go inside."

I followed Dawn through the secured doors, down a long white corridor and into one of the labs.

"You said something about a list?"

Pulling it from my satchel, I handed it to her. After a quick examination, she scanned it into a computer, tapped a few keys, and then looked back at me.

"This shouldn't take long. I'm cross-referencing to determine which ones on your list cause negative interactions with Zoloft." She walked to a nearby mini-fridge and retrieve a Dr. Pepper. "Do you want a Coke?" After having worked together in Haithem's absence, she knew my weakness. I nodded.

"I heard you bought a building not far from here."

"Where'd you hear that?"

"The grapevine, you know. The neighborhood is tight down here. Some people are excited to see what you do with the place."

"Them and me, both. Clive's got many plans."

"Are you gutting the place?"

"For the most part. You know how these old buildings are. The electric and plumbing needs a complete update."

"Ouch. That's costly."

"Yes, it is."

She turned to check progress on the computer, pressed a button, and a printer in the corner whirred, then spat out a single sheet of paper.

"There you go." She said, pointing to the printer.

After reviewing the paper, I tucked it into the side of my bag.

"Thanks for this, Dawn."

"Anytime, Dez. Good luck!"

THE MEDIA FRENZY OUTSIDE the Castle's house had died down since Thursday. From what I understood from reading the news, Rick Castle's bond was set at one million dollars, and so far, he was still in county lock-up. His employer was quick to distance themselves from him as news about what he'd allegedly been doing surfaced. I supposed they had to draw the line somewhere.

As I sat outside their place debating with myself about confronting Patricia with what I knew, I found it amusing that someone like Castle didn't have a get out of jail free card. Sometimes the system worked. Part of me thought about handing over my newly connected dots to the police. But if I did that, I wouldn't get the satisfaction of hearing her admit it to me after all her lies.

I knocked on the front door. When no one answered, I rang the bell. I knew Patricia Castle was home, so I rang the bell a few more times. Still no answer. It was a Saturday night, so their teens were probably out with friends. I tried the handle. It was unlocked, so I pushed the door open.

"Patricia?" I said, peering in with just my head peeking around the door. Nothing but silence greeted me.

"Patricia, it's Dez. Everything all right?" I stepped into the foyer, scanning the living room to my left, and the stairway ahead of me. A knot formed in the pit of my stomach. It was the same reaction I always had when shit was about to go sideways.

I crept through the front of the house slowly and found my way to the kitchen. All the lights were out. As I opened the basement door to check for activity, a cat sped past me almost taking me out at the ankles. Startled, I caught myself before tripping forward toward the railing.

"Damn cat."

Moving back to the front of the house, I climbed the stairs.

"Patricia, it's Dez. Are you okay?"

After checking each of the four bedrooms, the bathrooms, and the laundry room, I returned to the main level and re-entered the kitchen. From there, I could see they had a swimming pool and hot tub, both covered. To the far left in their yard, tucked beneath a large oak tree, was a shed. I walked outside, making a beeline for it. Yanking the door open, steam rolled out, obstructing my visibility. As it cleared, I saw Patrica Castle on the floor of the sauna.

"Shit! Patricia!"

Rushing inside, I crouched beside her limp body, searching for a pulse. Not finding one at her wrists, my fingers searched beneath her chin. It was weak. Shoving my hands beneath her shoulders, I hoisted her upper body up and began dragging her out, then set her down on the lawn. Fumbling in my bag, I located my phone and dialed 911.

"THESE THE PILLS YOU saw last time you were here?" Detective McDonough held up a bottle for me to examine. I'd moved to the outdoor dining set on the Castle's patio to get out of the way of the paramedics.

"Yes. They were on that table in the entryway." I handed him the report from Dawn Ryker. "Tegretol doesn't play nicely with Zoloft."

"The anti-depressant Libby Walker was taking." Detective Halliday said.

"I think Patricia Castle used it to make it look like Libby committed suicide. Zoloft side effects aren't pleasant, and Libby might have thought she was just having an adverse reaction to her new medication. She had only been taking it one or two months. I also read that if a Zoloft dosage is changed or a new drug is added, that could lead to something called Serotonin Syndrome."

"And that's fatal?"

"No, not all the time, but that, combined with whatever Rick Castle's device was doing to her, was more than enough to make Libby unstable, confused, and agitated. She might not have thought to call for help."

"How did Patricia Castle know about Libby Walker's medication?"

"I know she met with her at least once. Maybe during that meeting she saw Libby's pills. Maybe they met in her apartment."

"That's a lot of maybes, Jackson."

"That's why we pay you the big bucks. Am I free to go?"

Chapter Twenty-Nine

A WEEK AFTER FINDING Patricia Castle in her sauna, she'd been released from the hospital and taken into custody by OPD. Now she and her husband were both residents of the county. Cynthia had called to let me know that it looked like Patricia could post bail. So, she'd be out until her trial, but Rick Castle wasn't going anywhere.

I'd just arrived at the warehouse to go over plans with Clive. We hadn't talked much about the case recently because he'd been preoccupied with the building renovation effort.

"So, wait a minute. You're saying the old white lady slipped pills to Libby Walker and that killed her? I thought the dude killed her?"

"I think it was a bit of both. My buddy in the coroner's office said they found traces of Tegretol in Libby's system after they exhumed her body."

"Yeah, but how'd she get Libby to take it?"

"A smoothie."

"What? Get outa here."

"They think she offered Libby a smoothie laced with Tegretol, but they still don't know how she knew about Libby taking Zoloft."

"That is some messed up shit. What's going to happen to their kids?"

"They've moved to stay with family, from what I understand."

Clive thumbed through the blueprints.

"That's crazy. Why not just kick him to the curb?"

"Good question."

"It don't matter now though. They both screwed."

The faint clicks of heels tapping the floor got our attention. I turned to see Katrina walking toward us. She wore a black and gray pinstriped suit with wide-legged pants, and her blonde hair was pulled back, exposing her sharp jawline.

"Dez."

"What are you doing here?"

"I heard you were here."

"Really?"

"What's this?" She pulled a check from her jewel-toned clutch bag.

"It looks to me like you got my message."

"It was just a small favor between friends."

"You see, that's where we part ways. You agreed to stay away from Clive, and I agreed not to beat your ass. You remember that conversation, right?"

"You're all hat and no cattle, as they say." She smirked. "But it's one of the many reasons I love you."

"Keep your money, Katrina. We don't need it."

"If you insist, but you know where to find me if you change your mind. The place is shaping up nicely." She said slowly, surveying the surroundings. "It'll be nice having you closer."

"Just keep your shit out of my space and everything'll be fine."

"I wouldn't dream of impeding your progress, Dez. You're like a sister to me, you know that."

"Yeah, I know that."

She turned to leave saying, "Give Murphy my love. I hear he's around, again." Katrina left with a backhanded wave of her hand, and the door slammed behind her.

THE AROMA OF FRESH-baked naan, tandoori chicken, and Basmati rice greeted me when I opened the door. Setting my satchel on the side table, and hanging my jacket on the hook, I inspected the living room. Murphy had outdone himself. The coffee table had a tablecloth with two place settings and a bud vase with a single rose. A few IPAs nestled in an ice bucket sat nearby. And he'd set Star Trek, the Chris Pine version, to play on the TV.

Godfrey wasn't anywhere to be seen, so I assumed he was outside. Murphy peeked his head out from the kitchen.

"Just in time. Everything's ready."

He announced this as though he'd cooked the meal. Murphy was a takeout guy one hundred percent.

"What's the occasion?" I asked, slipping off my boots.

"Nothing." He walked into the living room balancing the food on two trays I didn't know I owned, stopping to kiss my forehead as he walked past. "Come on, we don't want it to get cold."

As we enjoyed our food and watched the movie, I felt comfortable, like I could get used to having Murphy around. I leaned against the couch, tucking my toes beneath his left thigh. His hand fell to my ankle, stroking it. The whole thing was so... normal. He caught me looking at him.

"What?"

"You're leaving again, aren't you?"

He sighed.

Thank you!

IF YOU ENJOYED READING Tempus, please consider leaving a review wherever you purchased your copy. Your kind and thoughtful review helps other readers find my work, and I appreciate that very much! Be sure to join Sinfully Scandalous readers everywhere at KoriDMiller.com. Catch up with me on Facebook[1].

1. http://www.facebook.com/authorkoridmiller

Photo © 2022 by the author

KORI D. MILLER WRITES the Sinfully Scandalous Mysteries and the Deadly Sins series at a tiny, narrow desk in her living room. Inspired by a small, but mighty collection of Funko Pops, Kori creates masterfully twisted plots for your entertainment. She's also the creative mind behind Kori's Clubhouse Books. Kori and her family reside in Nebraska where winter is bone cold, and summers are so hot you can bake cookies on your dashboard.

Don't miss out!

Visit the website below and you can sign up to receive emails whenever Kori D. Miller publishes a new book. There's no charge and no obligation.

https://books2read.com/r/B-A-OKYJ-JXPFB

BOOKS 2 READ

Connecting independent readers to independent writers.

Also by Kori D. Miller

A Dezeray Jackson Short Read
Deadly Sins I
Deadly Sins II
Deadly Sins III

Sinfully Scandalous Mysteries
Hush: A Dezeray Jackson Novel
North Downing: A Dezeray Jackson Novel
Tempus: A Dezeray Jackson Novel

Standalone
My Life in Black and White

Watch for more at https://www.koridmiller.com.

About the Publisher

Established in 2014, Back Porch Writer Press publishes adult, young adult, middle grade, and children's fiction and non-fiction. Our current list includes mystery, memoir, and science fiction titles.

www.ingramcontent.com/pod-product-compliance
Lightning Source LLC
Chambersburg PA
CBHW020420260626
47156CB00007B/2475